You'll have a great time getting to know the beauties of Mesa Blue! Best gal pals, these women share it all—from facials to low-fat-but-yummy recipes to tips on handling a difficult boss. And what kind of girlfriends would they be if they didn't spill their best dating stories!

Ultimately, it's one friend's strong desire to be a mother that has the threesome putting their lovely heads together. They're consulting the fabulous relationship advice book **2001 WAYS TO WED** to find a marriage-worthy man for...

Daisy Redford: Her biological clock puts Big Ben to shame! Could one unforgettable "indiscretion" bring her the little darling—and husband—she so desires?
Kiss a Handsome Stranger,
by Jacqueline Diamond, May 2001

Phoebe Lane: She's the head-turning hottie all men want, but she's staying single. Will she loosen the grasp on her independence for an older man?
Tame an Older Man,
by Kara Lennox, April 2001

Elise Foster: Her family is driving "the marriage bus" at high speed—and headed straight for Elise! She's running for cover, straight into the arms of her pretend fiancé, secret millionaire James Dillon.
Read on to see how their heartwarming story unfolds....

Dear Reader,

Welcome to Harlequin American Romance...where each month we offer four wonderful new books bursting with love!

Linda Randall Wisdom kicks off the month with *Bride of Dreams*, the latest installment in the RETURN TO TYLER series, in which a handsome Native American lawman is undeniably drawn to the pretty and mysterious new waitress in town. Watch for the Tyler series to continue next month in Harlequin Historicals. Next, a lovely schoolteacher is in for a big surprise when she wakes up in a hospital with no memory of her past—or how she'd gotten pregnant. Meet the last of the three identical sisters in Muriel Jensen's WHO'S THE DADDY? series in *Father Found*.

Bestselling author Judy Christenberry's *Rent a Millionaire Groom* launches Harlequin American Romance's new series, 2001 WAYS TO WED, about three best friends searching for Mr. Right who turn to a book guaranteed to help them make it to the altar. IDENTITY SWAP, Charlotte Douglas's new cross-line series, debuts with *Montana Mail-Order Wife*. In this exciting story, two women involved in a train accident switch identities and find much more than they bargained for. Follow the series next month in Harlequin Intrigue.

Enjoy this month's offerings, and make sure to return each and every month to Harlequin American Romance!

Wishing you happy reading,

Melissa Jeglinski
Associate Senior Editor
Harlequin American Romance

JUDY CHRISTENBERRY

Rent a Millionaire Groom

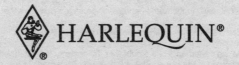

HARLEQUIN®

TORONTO • NEW YORK • LONDON
AMSTERDAM • PARIS • SYDNEY • HAMBURG
STOCKHOLM • ATHENS • TOKYO • MILAN • MADRID
PRAGUE • WARSAW • BUDAPEST • AUCKLAND

Special thanks and acknowledgment are given to
Judy Christenberry for her contribution
to the 2001 WAYS TO WED series.

ISBN 0-373-16867-5

RENT A MILLIONAIRE GROOM

Visit us at www.eHarlequin.com

Printed in U.S.A.

ABOUT THE AUTHOR

Judy Christenberry has been writing romances for fifteen years because she loves happy endings as much as her readers. Judy quit teaching French recently and devoted her time to writing. She hopes readers have as much fun reading her stories as she does writing them. She spends her spare time reading, watching her favorite sports teams and keeping track of her two daughters. Judy's a native Texan, but now lives in Arizona.

Books by Judy Christenberry

HARLEQUIN AMERICAN ROMANCE

555—FINDING DADDY
579—WHO'S THE DADDY?
612—WANTED: CHRISTMAS MOMMY
626—DADDY ON DEMAND
649—COWBOY CUPID*
653—COWBOY DADDY*
661—COWBOY GROOM*
665—COWBOY SURRENDER*
701—IN PAPA BEAR'S BED
726—A COWBOY AT HEART
735—MY DADDY THE DUKE
744—COWBOY COME HOME*
755—COWBOY SANTA
773—ONE HOT DADDY-TO-BE?†
777—SURPRISE—YOU'RE A DADDY!†
781—DADDY UNKNOWN†
785—THE LAST STUBBORN COWBOY†
802—BABY 2000
817—THE GREAT TEXAS WEDDING BARGAIN†
842—THE $10,000,000 TEXAS WEDDING†
853—PATCHWORK FAMILY
867—RENT A MILLIONAIRE GROOM

*4 Brides for 4 Brothers
†Tots for Texans

When three best friends
need advice on finding
that perfect love match they turn to
the wisest relationship book around...

2001 WAYS TO WED

You've probably dreamed about your wedding
since you were a girl. Was your someday wedding
a lavish event fit for a princess, or an intimate,
candlelit ceremony at a town-square church?
You likely imagined a dress to die for and a ring
with endless glitter. What song would mark your
first dance as man and wife?

Back then, the wedding was of more interest
than the *groom*. Boys were...well...*icky*. As a woman,
your feelings about the opposite sex have come
a long way from "icky"—you like men! So much,
in fact, that you'd like to spend your life with one.

This book offers rock-solid advice about getting
on the path to a happy marriage. First, you've got to
stop treating the dating scene like a grab bag,
taking the first "prize" you get your hands on.
You're a beautiful, talented, giving woman—
and there's an equally wonderful man out there
for you. And with 2001 WAYS TO WED,
you're sure to find—and marry—him!

Prologue

Elise Foster paused outside the front window of The Prickly Pear, spotting her two best friends through the plate glass.

The three of them were so different. Phoebe was a tall, beautiful blonde, the kind of woman men noticed. Not that they could ignore Daisy, with her auburn hair and vibrant smile. Elise considered herself to be average in looks compared to the other two, but tonight she had the answer to their problem.

With a pleased smile, she swung open the door and entered their favorite meeting place, a café and bar near Mesa Blue, the condominium complex where they all lived. "Sorry I'm late," she said by way of a greeting.

"No problem," Phoebe said with a grin. "We've been looking for potential candidates."

"And?" Elise asked, wondering if her solution might not be needed.

Daisy didn't smile. "Nothing. No one."

"Daisy, maybe you're being too...too choosey," Phoebe said gently. "You know, there really aren't any Prince Charmings out there. Just ordinary guys."

Daisy stared her friend down. "Maybe not, but he should at least make me want—want him."

"She's got you there," Elise agreed. Her friend had recently visited her doctor. After suffering from endometriosis for years, Daisy had to get pregnant in the very near future if she was ever to have a child. And she desperately wanted a baby.

That's why Phoebe and Elise were trying to help her, in spite of their own reluctance to march down the aisle. So far they'd had no luck.

Elise put a package on the table. "I have a solution."

Her friends stared at the small shopping bag and then at her.

Daisy leaned forward. "I had someone a little taller in mind, Elise."

Elise grinned in return. "That's the solution to *finding* the man, silly, not the man himself."

"Whew, that's a relief," Phoebe said with a chuckle. "I thought maybe you'd found a store named Daddys Are Us, or something."

"I wish I had. It would make things easier. No, I stopped by the bookstore on the way here."

Her friends rolled their eyes.

"Like that's unusual," Phoebe muttered.

Ignoring them, Elise pulled a book from the bag. "Ta-da!"

Both women leaned closer, staring at the title, *2001 WAYS TO WED*.

"You're kidding, right?" Phoebe demanded. "You bought one of those books that tells you never to go out without your makeup? To learn how to cook gourmet meals and always agree with whatever he says?''

''No, this book is different. It's—it's sensible.''

Daisy pulled the book from Elise's grasp and opened it.

''Well?'' Phoebe asked as she leaned over to look, too.

''It does seem to be practical. It says to smile a lot. To be positive. To think good thoughts about yourself.'' Daisy chewed on her bottom lip as she studied the words.

Elise noticed several men with their attention fixed on Daisy, clearly intrigued by her. That was why the entire campaign seemed ridiculous. Men wanted Daisy, but so far Daisy hadn't come up with a man she wanted.

Phoebe had suggested she and Elise help by introducing any men they knew. Unfortunately, Elise didn't know many men. She'd sworn off them a long time ago. And the only man in the Foreign Language Department at Arizona State University where she taught was Herr Gutenberg. At 5 foot 6 inches, with no hair, the 60-year-old wasn't the man for Daisy.

Their favorite waiter, George, arrived at the table. ''Hey, Elise, what can I bring you?''

''A diet cola, George. I've got to keep a clear mind tonight.'' That was a running joke, since Elise always ordered a diet cola.

''Aha, big doin's this evening?''

''Yep. We're on a search.''

George, assuming she was joking, said, ''Well, if you find the meaning of life, let me know.'' Then he took their orders and headed for the kitchen.

When they were alone once more, Elise said, "We'll all three study this book. Surely, then, we'll be able to find the perfect candidate for Daisy."

"And maybe for both of you, too," Daisy added, a hopeful smile on her face.

"No, thank you," Phoebe and Elise said together.

They both laughed. Then Phoebe added, "Some people aren't meant to be married, sweetie. I'm one of those."

"And I have my career to think of, you know," Elise added. "No, we'll help you, but we're not interested in husbands."

Chapter One

Elise Foster hung up the phone and ran a hand frustratedly through her hair. Her mother was going to drive her crazy. As the eldest of seven sisters, Elise had lived through five weddings featuring her sisters. Now Sharon, the baby, was getting married.

Her mother was concerned about Elise's old-maid status. And she'd urged her other daughters to talk to Elise about her solitary state, also. It seemed at least one of them called every day.

The situation hadn't been helped when she received a wedding invitation in the mail yesterday from her ex-fiancé.

Their engagement had ended twelve years ago, at the end of Elise's senior year in college. She'd discovered Richard wasn't interested in her, just in a good hostess for his blossoming career. She, of course, wasn't expected to have a career. It might interfere with his.

Even the fact that this was his second wedding didn't settle her stomach. Nor did the fact that she didn't want a husband.

But she wanted a fiancé badly.

That thought had been running around her mind for several days. A fiancé—temporary, of course—would get her sisters and her mother off her back. And she wouldn't feel she had to justify choosing to be alone every time she was introduced to someone new at her sister's wedding.

If she had a best friend, a hunk, hanging around, she'd ask him to do her a favor and pretend for a few days that he couldn't live without her.

But all her friends were female.

With a sigh she settled back in her chair. Her gaze lit on the book she'd bought, *2001 WAYS TO WED.* If she were searching for a real husband...but she wasn't. She had kept the book, however, to study it before she passed it over to Phoebe.

Maybe she should ''hire'' a fiancé. But that would mean going to an escort service. She'd heard those places were...distasteful. Besides, she wanted someone who would draw envy from her sisters. She wanted Prince Charming.

She picked up the book and idly flipped through it. She'd already read it several times. Then, suddenly, she sat upright in her chair. Of course. Why hadn't she thought of that before?

The chapter entitled ''Don't Forget Your Neighbors'' had given her an idea. She didn't have any neighbors at home who would do. But at work, that was another matter. ASU had an excellent Drama Department. She could hire a starving actor to be her fiancé.

She hurried from her office. One of her fellow professors, Dr. Grable, had worked with the Drama Department last semester when they'd been producing one of Molière's plays. Maybe she could recommend someone.

Several hours later, after teaching her two o'clock class and delicately questioning Cecille Grable, Elise took a deep breath and headed for the Drama Department.

Cecille's response kept playing in her mind. *"Well, if you're looking for what the young ladies today call a hunk, I'd recommend Bobby Dillon. He's a teaching assistant, a little older than the college students, but he grabs the eye. If one is interested in such things."* Cecille, nearing retirement age, had a twinkle in her eye that told Elise even *she* was still interested in such things.

Elise opened the door to the semi-dark auditorium and slid into the last row of seats, hoping her eyes would adjust quickly to the dim light. On stage, a number of students were going through their lines.

How was she going to identify the young man? And heavens, she hoped he didn't look too young. There were several handsome young men on stage, but—

"Repeat that line. I couldn't hear it at all."

The deep, silky voice that gave the command came from the center of the auditorium. Elise hadn't noticed the man slumped down in his chair.

The voice alone made him perfect for her needs. He could read the telephone directory and she'd be enthralled. No wonder he was in the Drama Department. He had a great future ahead of him.

Of course, she also hoped he was handsome. But Cecille had said—

The house lights came up and the man stood. Tall,

broad-shouldered, trim. So far so good. Elise quickly rose and hurried down the aisle, determined to catch him before he moved to the stage and they had an audience.

"Mr. Dillon?" she called softly.

He'd just reached the end of the row of seats and he spun around, as if startled. With a frown, he replied, "Yes?"

"May I have a word with you?"

He didn't look any too happy, so she quickly added, "It's about a job."

He stared at her, and she felt her cheeks flush. She wasn't used to such concentrated interest. He began, "The normal channels—"

"It's—it's personal. I mean, I don't need you to appear on stage, but—it's rather difficult to explain. I'll be glad to buy you a cup of coffee while I try to make it clear. I haven't figured out how much to offer you, but I'm sure we can come to an agreement."

"You're offering *me* a job?"

His surprise didn't make sense, unless it was caused by his pride. "Why, yes. Please don't be embarrassed. I understand acting jobs aren't too plentiful unless you're in Hollywood." He continued to stare at her. "You are Bobby Dillon, aren't you?"

His eyes seemed to widen. Then, after a quick look over his shoulder, he said, "Yes, that's me. I'm—I'm Bobby Dillon."

And Cecille had been right. He was perfect. "If you don't want to go to the Student Union, there's a coffee shop a couple of blocks over. Shall I meet you there in—'' she paused to look at her watch ''—fifteen minutes?''

''All right,'' he agreed.

She stuck out her hand to seal the agreement, almost afraid he wouldn't show. ''I'll see you there.''

''Yes,'' he agreed.

She could feel his gaze on her as she walked out of the auditorium, and for the first time in her life she wished she had Phoebe's knockout looks.

She wasn't much of a match for the Prince Charming she'd just found.

JAMES DILLON STARED at the young woman walking away. Her neat figure would attract almost any man, but it was the anxious expression in her green eyes that had caught his attention.

That and the offer of a job.

He chuckled, a sound not often heard of late. There hadn't been a lot to laugh about. Which explained why he was hanging out on campus, visiting his brother, the apparently famous Bobby Dillon.

''Who was that?'' Bobby asked, coming up behind him.

''I'm not sure.''

Bobby shrugged. ''Well, thanks for helping me out. I was pretty sure Sandy wasn't projecting, but I needed to be on stage to keep the pace going.''

''Glad to be of assistance.'' James was barely following Bobby's words. He couldn't stop thinking about the woman. She wasn't a student—not dressed in that suit. Her light brown hair had been pulled back with a clasp, small gold earrings on her ears. Nothing flashy, suggestive or even inviting.

The opposite of Sylvia, his ex-wife, thank God.

"So, I'll see you later?" Bobby asked, turning back toward the stage. "Or you're welcome to hang around for the next class, if you want."

"Uh, no, thanks, I've got—got some things to do. See you later."

Bobby called an agreement over his shoulder, leaving James free to concentrate on the mystery woman.

Her request had seemed really important to her. Of course, he knew it was unfair to let her think he was Bobby. After he heard her offer, he'd probably have to confess his lie. But just for a while, for an hour, he could be someone other than James Dillon, wealthy businessman, pursued by women all over Arizona.

Lately, being James Dillon hadn't been much fun.

So dressed in jeans, tennis shoes, a short-sleeved knit shirt with the shirttail hanging out, he'd come to see Bobby.

He checked his watch. He'd have to hurry to make the fifteen-minute deadline. And it suddenly seemed important to find out exactly what Miss Green Eyes wanted.

Because he was a sucker for green eyes.

ELISE HAD GONE straight to the coffee shop, needing time to pull herself together and go over her proposal. The man was perfect, and she didn't want to mess things up. Now that she'd seen him, the half-baked plan had become a necessity.

Her sisters would die. He was handsome, as Cecille had said—but there was more. He carried an air of authority that commanded attention. Her thoughts flew to her ex-fiancé, Richard. He'd be apoplectic with jealousy.

That thought pleased her, even as she acknowledged its pettiness. Why Bobby hadn't been discovered professionally yet, she didn't know. But she could predict a brilliant future for him in Hollywood.

Something caused her to look up, and she almost forgot to breathe. He stood by the table, waiting for her to invite him to join her. "Oh, hi!" she said, realizing she sounded as breathy and enthralled as a freshman girl talking to the senior football star.

She cleared her throat. "Won't you sit down?"

That was better, more professional.

He smiled, and she had to take another deep breath. She figured his value just doubled.

"Thanks. You know me, but I haven't met you before, have I? What's your name?"

Her cheeks flamed. "Oh, I'm so sorry. I was intent on getting you to listen to me. I forgot to introduce myself. I'm Dr. Elise Foster, French professor at the school."

"I'm delighted to meet you."

"Thank you, Bobby," she said, letting out her pent-up breath. He looked older and somehow more sophisticated than the college students. But he was a teaching assistant, she remembered, so he had to be in advanced graduate studies.

He frowned, and she wondered what she'd said wrong.

"Would you mind calling me James? Bobby is a stage name. Unless I need it for the job you're offering."

"Of course, James. I mean, it won't be necessary if you— Yes, that's fine."

The waitress appeared beside the table, distracting them. Elise ordered a diet cola, but James opted for coffee.

"Do you want anything to eat? A piece of pie, French fries, a hamburger?" she offered. After all, actors were notoriously broke. Maybe he hadn't eaten in a while.

"No thanks, just coffee."

As soon as the waitress left, he leaned forward, loosely clasping his hands together on the table.

She loved his hands. Well-tended, the fingers were long but strong, powerful. She also noticed he wore no wedding ring. She hadn't even thought to ask about that.

"You're not married, are you?" she asked hurriedly.

One dark eyebrow rose over clear blue eyes. "This...offer is getting more interesting by the minute."

She blushed again. "No! I didn't mean— It might complicate things if— Never mind."

"No, I'm not married."

"Oh, good." At least he hadn't run out of the coffee shop in horror. She wasn't managing to sound as in control as she'd planned, but he was still here.

"Why does it matter?"

"Well, I told you the job was—was personal. I don't want you to get the wrong idea, but I need an escort."

That fascinating brow rose again. "I can't believe you have difficulty finding an escort, Dr. Foster."

"Um, make it Elise. It's not— I don't date much."

"Your choice, I'm sure."

That was flattering, but considering all the weeks they'd worked trying to find a man for Daisy, she wasn't sure it was accurate. The thought of Daisy made her feel guilty. Should she introduce her friend to Bobby—James? No, an actor wasn't in a stable job situation. That wouldn't do at all for a prospective father.

That rationalization made her feel much better.

"Are we talking about a class reunion?" he guessed. "I've heard of people taking pretend partners to those things to impress their classmates."

He was taking everything very well, but Elise hated the conversation. She would never do that, lie to impress someone. That had been Richard's standard M.O.

But that's what you're doing, isn't it? a small voice inside her asked. *No, I'm lying to get some peace from my family.* She needed to make sure that James understood that.

"It's not a reunion." She licked her suddenly dry lips. "You see, I come from a large family."

"Lucky you."

She blinked, surprised by his response. "Don't you have brothers and sisters?"

"One brother. But there's eleven years difference between us, so it was almost like being an only child."

"Oh. Well, I guess there are advantages to a large family, though some days it's hard to remember them."

He smiled again, and she figured he'd make his

fortune on the basis of his smile alone. Or his eyes. His Paul Newman blue eyes crinkled slightly at the corners.

"Um, yes, well, I have six sisters and one brother."

"So there are eight of you. That's quite a large family these days."

She felt as if she was babbling, and she'd had everything planned out so rationally. "Yes," she agreed, and clamped her mouth shut.

That eyebrow again. He looked at her, waiting for her to continue.

"Sharon, my baby sister, is getting married soon."

"The youngest? How old is she?"

"Twenty-two. She finished college in December."

He frowned, and she caught her breath. "You and your sisters must've been born close together because you don't look much older."

He was good with the flattery. She supposed it must be his stock-in-trade. "I'm thirty-three. My brother is older."

"And you already have your doctorate? I'm impressed. Did you study in France?"

"Yes, at the— Never mind," she hurriedly said. If she wasn't careful, she'd get distracted and never tell him what she really wanted.

"You want to stick to the subject?" he asked, smiling again, a twinkle in his eye.

With a sigh, she said, "Yes, please. This is difficult enough as it is."

"To ask me to escort you to your sister's wedding? That's not asking much. I'll be glad to take you."

Elise seriously considered accepting his offer. Then she could tell him just before the wedding that she actually needed him to appear to be more than just her date—but that would be wrong.

With another sigh, she said, "Thank you, but that's not exactly what I'm asking." She cleared her throat and tried again. "I'm asking you to be my fiancé."

Chapter Two

He couldn't believe it.

He'd been suckered in, like an inexperienced teen-ager.

Damn it, he was thirty-six. He'd been chased by the best, and he'd fallen for this green-eyed witch's simple plan.

He schooled his features to give nothing away. "I'm not interested in marriage, Dr. Foster."

As he started to rise, her hand reached across the table and grabbed his wrist. He didn't know whether to believe the look of horror on her face. If she was acting, she was damn good.

"No! I mean, neither am I!"

He raised his eyebrow again, still not convinced it wasn't a trap. Too many women had seen his millions as a ticket to easy street.

"I meant I want you to come to the wedding as my *pretend* fiancé. I only need you until after the wedding. I like being single. I have my career. It's only a pretense!"

She sounded desperate, he'd give her that. But he didn't see why it would be so important to her...unless she had an ulterior motive. "Why is it necessary?"

"Look, I... Oh, never mind. It was a crazy idea. I'll figure out something."

Now it was his turn to reach out and stop her from rising. Was he crazy? He was backing away from the exit sign. "Just explain. You owe me that, at least."

Her cheeks were red from what might have been embarrassment and she kept her gaze lowered, denying him the sight of those beautiful green eyes. A strand of hair, curling slightly, had escaped the clasp and dangled beside her cheek, urging him to tuck it behind her ear. Most of all, her full pink lips, without lipstick, trembled.

"I'm tired of being harassed," she muttered.

"Harassed? By whom?"

"My family!" she almost shouted, her eyes blazing with what appeared to be anger as she finally looked at him. "They won't leave me alone. I chose not to marry. Not to be a—a satellite to some man. I have my own career and I'm happy with my life. But they won't leave me alone!"

The cold anger in his own heart eased slightly. He was beginning to believe her again. "What do they do?"

"You mean other than calling me every day to suggest I'm a loser old maid with no prospects?" she returned, sarcasm having replaced the anger.

"Every day?"

"I have six sisters plus my mother. And she has two sisters. My grandmother died last year, so she can't join in—but she would if she could."

"No wonder you weren't enthusiastic about large families," he said, relaxing a little more.

Tears pooled in her eyes. "I love my family. But—but they're driving me crazy!"

Leaning forward, he captured her hands in his. "But, Elise, this would only be a temporary solution. Then what?"

"You don't understand. It's the prospect of a wedding that stirs them all up. And this is the last wedding. Every sister will be married. There won't be any more weddings on the horizon to get them excited. Chance, my brother, certainly won't be marching down the aisle. So if I can just get through this one, I'll be okay."

"Are you sure?"

"Yes. I don't see them all that often. For several months after the wedding I can tell them you've gotten a role in Hollywood. Then I'll tell them we can't marry because you're always gone. It's simple."

James didn't quite believe her last statement. But the prospect of pretending to be Elise's fiancé had some appeal for him. A great deal of appeal, actually. He was fascinated by her emotion, her soft lips, her green eyes.

Recognizing a danger signal when he saw it, he let go of her hands and sat back. "When is the wedding?"

"In three weeks. That would be enough time to—to learn about each other, wouldn't it? I mean, I can write out everything you'd have to know."

Her scholarly approach tickled him. She thought she could write a report and they could convince everyone they were lovers? He grinned. "Well, now,

I'm a method actor, sweetheart. I'd have to spend time with you to do a good job.''

The reluctance on her face assured him he'd been wrong about Elise Foster. She wasn't trying to marry him. She didn't even want to date him. Which only made her more attractive.

"Spend time? How much time? I mean, I have my classes and office hours and grading papers. I can't—''

"Evenings, Elise. I have work to do, too. But we could spend a few evenings together, have dinner, talk…you know, like a real couple.''

She looked lost. He understood. He hadn't dated anyone on a regular basis in years. He hadn't been comfortable enough with a woman to let her get that close. Was he making another mistake?

"I suppose we could…spend a few evenings together.''

"Okay, you've got a deal.'' He extended his hand across the table.

After hesitating, she put her hand in his. "But we haven't discussed your fee.''

"That's not necessary.'' In fact, he was wondering if he should offer to pay *her*. There was an excitement singing through his veins, an enthusiasm for the days ahead that he hadn't felt in some time.

"Of course, it's necessary. I'm hiring you. How much would you be paid for your time if you were doing a play?''

He had no idea what Bobby would receive, so he guessed. "Union wages are a hundred and twenty a day.''

She swallowed. "Okay. How—how many times will we need to go out?''

"Oh, you don't pay me for those evenings. That's research. I'm responsible for research. You only pay for the time at the wedding." He grinned, proud of his solution.

"No, that's not right. The wedding will be three days, but I'll pay half that rate for the evenings." She gave an abrupt nod, firmness in her lips.

He thought she looked adorable.

He shook his head, trying to dismiss that thought.

"No? You won't agree to half? Okay, I can pay full—"

"That's not what I meant! That's fine. What you said was fine. We'll settle up after the wedding." When it was over, he'd tell her who he really was. Payment wouldn't be necessary.

"But won't you need some money in advance?" She bit down on her bottom lip, and James longed to pull her to him, to touch her there.

"Uh, no, I'll be fine."

Her earnest, professorial look firmly in place, she said, "Look, James, don't let your pride get in the way. I know teaching assistants don't make much money. I'll write a check for five hundred dollars and you keep a list of expenses."

What could he say? He wanted that check. It was proof that she wasn't after his money, wasn't it? Not that he'd cash it. Instead, he'd probably frame it, to remember a certain green-eyed siren who had captured him...temporarily.

ELISE WAS UNSETTLED by her arrangement.

Or maybe she was unsettled by James's insistence that their first research evening be tonight.

Not that she'd had plans. No, she had intended to go over her lesson plans for the next day. And there was a test she needed to grade. Normal activities.

Or maybe she was unsettled by the excitement filling her. This wasn't a date! And even if it were, a date shouldn't cause such interest. After all, a male friend was no different from a female one.

That blatant lie couldn't sail past her truth alarm without ringing wildly. Okay, so sitting across from James Dillon, date or not, was a lot different from sitting with Phoebe and Daisy.

She didn't shampoo her hair for Phoebe and Daisy. Or shave her legs.

The phone rang.

"Hi," Phoebe sang out, her voice cheery. "I met a man today."

Elise gasped. She had? It must be catching.

"I'm going to introduce him to Daisy," Phoebe continued.

Oh. Big difference. Elise wasn't going to introduce the man she'd met to Daisy. Because he wasn't right for her.

"That's great. Have you told Daisy?"

"Nope. I thought we'd all grab a bite to eat at The Prickly Pear and discuss it. You can help me convince her."

"Tonight?" Elise almost squeaked, then cleared her throat to sound normal. "Uh, I can't tonight."

"Why not?"

"I'm, uh, doing research."

"For Daisy?"

"No! For me. I'm using the book to solve one of my problems."

"When are you going out?"

"At seven."

"Great, Daisy and I will be right over. We want to hear all about this research."

Before Elise could protest, Phoebe hung up. But it didn't matter. She'd have to tell her friends the truth, anyway, sooner or later. Better to get it out of the way.

She grabbed a quick shower, shampooed her hair. When she stepped out, the doorbell was ringing. "Coming!" she shouted as she dashed to her bedroom to find her silky robe. Then she let in her two friends.

"What's going on?" Daisy asked at once. "It sounds mysterious."

"No, it's not. Come in. I'll get us a cola." Elise figured she had half an hour before she needed to get ready. "I've figured out a way to stop my family from harassing me about my single state."

"That's hard to believe," Phoebe said. "Haven't they been making daily calls?"

"Yes. But I've found a fiancé."

Daisy almost dropped the drink Elise had just handed her. "What? You're engaged?"

"No, but the book said look around your neighborhood and—"

"You're hitting on Jeff? Elise, he's way too young for you," Phoebe interrupted. "Besides, I thought you didn't want to marry?"

Elise closed her eyes, knowing she'd made a mess of her explanation. Jeff was the guy who cleaned the pool at Mesa Blue. He was always flirting with all of them, but he was only twenty-two—a baby.

Just how old do you think James is? that irritating inner voice asked. She didn't want to think about that. Instead, she attempted to answer Phoebe.

"I don't want to marry. I'm telling this all wrong, just like I did this afternoon."

"You told someone else before you told us?" Daisy asked, hurt in her eyes.

"Well, I had to!" Elise exclaimed. "Otherwise he wouldn't have agreed to be my fiancé. My *pretend* fiancé!" she emphasized.

"Oh, this is good," Phoebe said, curling up on the sofa. "Tell us all about him."

And Elise did, providing the basic facts. Phoebe, however, thought she'd left something out.

"You haven't described him."

"Well, he's your typical Hollywood hunk." Elise hoped that would satisfy her friends. She should've known better.

After staring at her, Phoebe nodded her head and said, "I can't wait to meet him. Are you going to introduce him to Daisy afterwards?"

"No! Actors aren't—stable. I mean, their jobs aren't stable. That wouldn't be good for a prospective dad, you know."

"She's right," Daisy agreed, which settled Elise's nerves. "They're always gone. And they're notorious for having affairs with the women they work with."

Elise didn't like that thought. Not that it was any of her business what James did when he made movies. *If* he made movies.

Desperate to end the conversation before she revealed too much to herself as well as to her friends, she stood. "Look, I need to get ready. He's going to be here at seven."

"Want to let me do your makeup?" Phoebe asked.

Phoebe was a makeup consultant as well as a college student, a "retread" college student as she called herself, and she frequently offered to do Elise's makeup. Elise always refused.

"This isn't a date, Phoebe, but thank you. It's research. That's what James called it."

"Okay, come on, Daisy, and I'll tell you about the guy I found for you today over dinner at The Prickly Pear." Phoebe stood and offered a hand to pull Daisy to her feet.

Daisy joined Phoebe. "I wish you were coming with us, Elise."

"When I get in, I'll call you to find out what the two of you decided about the latest husband prospect for Daisy. With that book to help us, I'm sure you'll be married and expecting soon, Daisy."

"I hope so," Daisy said with a sigh.

JAMES COULDN'T BELIEVE how much he was looking forward to his evening with Elise. Dr. Elise Foster. His friends would laugh if they realized he was dating an egghead, an intellectual.

Not that he was dumb, but he'd made his money understanding popular culture. His ad agency had done some of the most successful ad campaigns in the past few years. That was a long way from Shakespeare, or maybe he should say Molière, the French answer to the famous English playwright.

And Bobby would probably come unglued. James

was pretty sure Bobby had taken French with Elise. He remembered now his brother talking about a beautiful French teacher. And Elise was beautiful, in a quiet way. Bobby had only stayed in the class one semester. Studying verb conjugations wasn't his cup of tea. He'd only wanted to pick up the proper accent.

That probably explained why Elise hadn't remembered his brother.

He dressed carefully, sticking with jeans and a casual shirt, topped by a linen sports coat. He took the check Elise had given him and tucked it in his breast pocket. His good luck charm.

Earlier, he'd convinced his housekeeper to swap cars with him for the evening. She hadn't wanted to drive his Mercedes, but she'd promised to visit her sister. If he turned up in the sleek black car, Elise would smell a rat for sure. So tonight, he was driving MaryBelle's inexpensive sedan.

He reminded himself to talk MaryBelle into allowing him to get the car tuned up for her. It was an older model car, and the rough sound of the engine had him concerned for MaryBelle's safety. His housekeeper was an energetic sixty-year-old, who could cook and clean like a demon. But she knew nothing about cars. If it broke down with her, she'd be stranded.

He parked in front of the condominiums where Elise lived. Mesa Blue. It actually had a front lawn, an unusual feature in Phoenix. Elise had said it got its name from the swimming pool, the center of the complex. Its tile bottom was a deep blue.

He approved of the well-lit area. It looked safe to

him. Funny, he'd never evaluated the security of his dates' homes before. It was probably because he'd been thinking about MaryBelle's safety. Yeah, that was it.

He found her apartment on the second floor, apartment 2D, and knocked. His heart rate sped up as he heard footsteps approaching.

When the door opened, he caught his breath.

Gone was the staid suit, the prim hairdo. Elise was dressed in jeans, as he was, topped by a green short-sleeved sweater with a modest V-neck. Her light brown hair was down, curving around her face, and she looked like a college student herself.

He found himself leaning forward, as if to kiss her hello, and stepped back. "Ready?" he asked hastily.

"Yes. Do you want to come in for a drink?"

"If you don't mind, no. I'm starving."

She immediately stepped out of her apartment and locked the door behind her. "Of course. Where shall we go?"

"I've found a place I think you'll like. I wanted somewhere quiet so we can talk. Some of these places have the music turned up so loud you can't hear yourself think."

Some of the tension he'd noted on her face eased. "I know what you mean. I thought you might prefer those kinds of places. You're—you're younger, I suppose."

"Actually, I'm not as young as you might think," he admitted, avoiding her gaze. "I came back to ASU after trying my luck on the job market. I discovered I'm more interested in creating drama than I am in acting." At least, that's what his brother

Bobby had told him when Bobby had made the decision to return to college after a couple of years in Los Angeles.

"Really? Do you write plays?"

"I'm working on a couple. Nothing that's been bought yet."

"That's wonderful, James," she said eagerly.

He wasn't sure why that news pleased her so, but he had no objection to making her happy. She was practically beaming at him.

"You prefer a playwright to an actor?"

Her cheeks flushed and she looked away. "It just seems more—more interesting, actually. One of my friends is creative. She has a gallery nearby called Native Art. But her greatest happiness comes when she creates her own art."

"Hey, I've been in that store. She has some nice stuff. And she's done some of it?" He put his hand on her back to guide her down the stairs, liking the warmth of her, a soft floral scent drifting to his nostrils.

"Actually, no. She creates pottery for her friends, but she won't put her own work in the store. She doesn't think it's good enough."

"Creative people are often unsure of themselves." He dealt with employees like Elise's friend. Brilliant people, but their mood swings sometimes made them difficult to work with.

"Are you?"

It took him a minute to figure out what she was asking. "Uh, I suppose we all are unsure of ourselves sometimes."

When he and Sylvia had divorced, the anger in

him had fueled his first few years, leaving him no room for self-doubt. By the time the anger had dissipated, he'd risen so high in the business, he had a history to fall back on. He hadn't thought of his past like that. Maybe he owed Sylvia, after all.

He chuckled, amused by his thoughts.

"What's funny?" Elise asked, as they reached the bottom of the stairs.

"Sorry. Your question reminded me of some of my early struggles."

"It's good that you can laugh at them."

"Yeah, it is." He hadn't laughed at them before. Elise was good for him.

"I hope you don't mind my car. It's not exactly elegant," he said, directing her to MaryBelle's car. He'd rather be driving his Mercedes.

"Of course, I don't mind. In fact, we can drive mine if you want."

"No, we'll take—mine. But what kind of car do you drive? I hope it's safe."

"Oh, yes. I've never had any trouble with it."

"Good," he agreed, and held open the door for her.

He got behind the wheel, glad he'd already adjusted the seat and the mirrors for his height. He backed out of the parking lot. "I like your condos. They look nice."

"Yes, they are. The people who live here are wonderful. My two best friends are here, but everyone's friendly."

He couldn't imagine anyone being unfriendly to Elise, especially men. "Any single men live here?"

"Well, there's Jeff and Bill."

He assured himself it was curiosity that had him asking, "Why didn't you ask one of them to be your pretend fiancé?"

She smiled at him. "Because Jeff is the same age as my students and Bill is almost old enough to be my father. Neither of them would be able to convince my sisters we were serious."

He nodded, accepting the implied compliment with a smile. "Well, I'll do my best to be convincing."

"I'm sure you will."

James saw the sign for the place he'd found earlier, having decided it would be perfect for a casual meal and conversation. Someplace where he wouldn't be recognized.

"Here we are," he said as he parked the car.

He turned to Elise, only to find her staring at the restaurant, her face pale.

Chapter Three

Elise stared at the familiar sign: The Prickly Pear. Out of all the restaurants in Phoenix, he'd chosen her favorite hangout? Where her friends were dining?

"Is something wrong? Don't you like this place?"

"Oh…yes, I love it. I come here often."

"Is that it? You're afraid you'll be seen with me?"

She heard the annoyance in his voice. With a smile, she said, "Are you kidding? Being seen with you will do wonders for my reputation."

Her words must've pleased him because he gave her that devastating smile and squeezed her hand.

"Good. I was afraid you had a boyfriend stashed away somewhere and didn't want him to see us out together."

He got out of the car and came around to open her door before she could pull herself together to get out. "A boyfriend?" she repeated. "If I had a boyfriend, why would I hire you?"

He was still smiling as he took her by the hand. "I guess you wouldn't."

"Um, Jeff, the guy who cleans the pool, might be bartending tonight. That's his part-time job. And—

and my friends Phoebe and Daisy were coming here for dinner. But there's no one else. I mean, I'm not hiding anyone.''

James held the door open for her, and she walked in. The hostess who normally worked there wasn't in sight. George, their usual waiter, saw her pausing by the door and came sailing by, a tray in his hands. He stooped and kissed her cheek.

"Hi, love. Just pick a table anywhere. You know the routine." Then he headed off to deliver the food on his tray.

Elise swallowed and turned to look at James. He had a curiously suspicious look on his face. "That's George. He usually waits on us."

"Yeah, I can tell you know him. Why didn't you ask *him?*''

Lowering her voice so no one could hear her, she said, "Because George is already married. He and his wife are attending school and working part time."

James took a deep breath. "Okay. Where do you want to sit."

Phoebe and Daisy had discovered them by that time and were waving from across the room. "Uh, my friends are here. Do you mind if we say hello?"

"Of course not. But I'd rather not join them tonight. We need to talk, to get to know each other."

"Yes, of course." She led the way to their table, glad they weren't going to have dinner with Phoebe and Daisy. James would only have eyes for her friends. They were so alive, so beautiful.

"Hi, Phoebe and Daisy. This is James Dillon.

James, these are my two best friends, Phoebe Lane and Daisy Redford.''

"Evening, ladies.''

Elise could tell how impressed her friends were with James. Which only reinforced her confidence in her excellent choice. Her sisters would be overwhelmed.

She smiled at her friends, pleased at their approval.

James's arm came around her shoulders, surprising her. His warmth, the scent of his aftershave, the thrill she experienced when he touched her, distracted her. And filled her with concern. She didn't want to become too interested in James Dillon.

"You know, Elise, why don't we join Phoebe and Daisy for dinner. Unless you two ladies object? Your food hasn't arrived yet?''

"No, we haven't even ordered," Daisy said. "George is rushed off his feet tonight.''

"Good, then how about it, Elise?'' James said, pulling out the nearest empty chair.

Her heart fell. He was attracted to her friends. Maybe it was Daisy who drew him. Then they wouldn't have to worry about finding a man for her. Or maybe it was Phoebe, with her starlet looks. James was probably used to starlets.

"Elise?''

"Oh, oh, yes, of course. That would be delightful.''

And she fell into the chair he held out for her.

JAMES THOUGHT ELISE had seemed very tense, until she smiled at her friends. So he'd decided Elise might be more forthcoming if she was relaxed.

Now he knew he'd miscalculated. She was more tense than ever. What had gone wrong?

He sat down next to her, trying to figure out how to get out of his decision.

George rushed up. "The usual, darlin's?"

Elise frowned. "James hasn't been here before. I don't know—"

"What's the usual?" he asked, not much caring what he ate. He was more interested in Elise.

"A chicken Caesar salad," Phoebe explained. "But their burgers are really good."

"I'll have a burger," he said at once.

George nodded in his direction. Then, after the three women said they'd have the usual, he moved on.

"So, you three must eat here a lot," he commented, hoping to see Elise relax.

"Several times a week," Daisy said. "After working all day, it doesn't seem worth the effort to cook for one when we can come here and have a healthy salad."

"I know what you mean. If I didn't have—" He broke off, reminding himself a struggling teaching assistant didn't have a housekeeper. "Uh, if I didn't have my mom nearby, I'd exist on hamburgers."

Phoebe chuckled. "I don't think a man ever outgrows his need to go home to be fed."

"Which one of you has the art gallery?" he asked.

Daisy looked at Elise, then back at James. "That's me."

"I've been to it. I was impressed with your inventory."

"Oh, thank you. You're interested in art?"

"Depends—but I liked what you had," he said.

The other two grinned in response to his flattery, but Elise did not.

It suddenly occurred to him that he didn't know just how much Elise had told her friends. Did she want them to think he was a serious suitor? "Uh, Elise and I just met. I thought if we joined you two, you could tell me secrets about her." He nudged Elise with his elbow, hoping to draw some response.

"They know," she said, not looking at him.

James cocked an eyebrow at the other two women. "You do?"

They nodded. Daisy added, "Elise told us because we're searching for a man for me, and she used the book to find you."

James sat back in his chair and stared at the three women. What was wrong with the men these three knew? They were all beautiful. Why did they have to search for men?

"Maybe you know more than I do. What book? And why are you searching for a man?" he finished, looking at Daisy.

Phoebe fielded the first question. *"2001 WAYS TO WED."*

When he stared at her blankly, she added, "That's the book."

James turned to Elise, whose cheeks were rosy red. "You found me in a book?"

"No, not exactly," Elise said. "It said to look at your neighbors. I told you there weren't any neighbors who would do, but when I thought about work, I remembered the Drama Department. It sounded like the perfect place to find someone who could—pretend.''

"Makes sense," he agreed. Then he turned to Daisy. "I know it's none of my business, but why are you looking for a man? I mean, why do you have to look? I would think any of you could have your choice of men."

"That's sweet of you," Phoebe said with a smile, "but Daisy is the only one looking."

"And it's because my biological clock is ticking," Daisy hurriedly added. "I'm ready to have a child."

James's eyes widened. "I think I'm glad I'm helping out Elise and not you."

"I'm not looking for anything temporary," Daisy said, squaring her jaw. "I was raised without a father. I won't do that to my child."

"Good for you," he agreed. Then he reached over and picked up Elise's hand. "How's your biological clock, sweetheart?"

Elise snatched her hand away. "Just fine, thank you. Remember all those sisters? Who do you think took care of them?"

"Your brother?" he teased, knowing the answer.

"Not hardly."

"I can't wait to meet this brother, raised with seven sisters. He's either overwhelmingly masculine, in self-defense, or he learned to play with dolls."

"Definitely the first," Elise said without hesitation.

James looked at the other two.

"We couldn't tell you," Phoebe said. "We've never met him. He doesn't come around often."

"He's an attorney and has long hours," Elise said. "I talk to him on the phone, but he doesn't have a lot of spare time."

"I guess his job is the reason you said he wouldn't be marching down the aisle anytime soon."

Elise nodded.

James knew most people would classify him in the same group. And they'd be right. Which explained why he'd questioned Elise's motives early on. But somehow he just didn't see deceit being her strong point.

"So, do you think Elise and I will be able to pull this thing off?"

He read the doubt on her friends' faces.

"Well, you have three weeks," Phoebe said. "And you're an actor. But I don't know about Elise."

"Hey! I can pretend," Elise protested.

Daisy chuckled. "You can't even pay an insincere compliment, Elise. She blushes a bright red when she tries," she added to James. "If we really want to know if we've bought something we shouldn't have, we ask Elise."

Elise scowled at Daisy, but James saw the concern in her gaze. "Don't worry, honey. I'll teach you method acting. You'll do fine." He knew that much from Bobby.

Phoebe chuckled. "Is that your style of acting?"

James knew she understood what he meant, but Elise still didn't have a clue. "It works best, especially for beginners."

Their dinners arrived at that moment. The food was good, the conversation even better.

James decided he'd learned more about Elise than he would have on their own. In particular, he noted her friends' remarks about her honesty.

Sylvia had been an expert liar.

Several hours later, the two friends excused themselves, both claiming chores that had to be done that evening before bedtime.

"I enjoyed meeting your friends, but they don't seem practical types—especially Phoebe," James said after they'd left.

"She's very beautiful."

"None of you are going to be used on wanted posters, sweetheart," he said with a chuckle. "But she seems more the movie-star type. Like maybe she's an actress, too."

"She was at one time, but her heart wasn't in it. She's…got other plans now."

"Interesting friends."

Elise said thanks, but she looked away.

"Are you upset that we joined them?"

"No, of course not," she hurriedly said, and smiled at him.

But it wasn't her best smile.

"I figured once you met them, you'd want to get to know them better," she said.

He stared at her. "Are you implying I'm more interested in them than I am in you?" He couldn't believe she'd think that.

"It doesn't matter. We're pretending, remember? I need to excuse myself. I'll be back in a minute."

James stared after her, confused.

"YOU IDIOT!" Elise addressed herself in the mirror. "You're the one who keeps forgetting. How could you let him know that you're jealous."

She powdered her nose and tried to get up the courage to return to the table. It had been an enlightening evening. For her. She'd discovered James had an infinite capacity for charm. And that she was way too interested in him.

What was she going to do now? Start over?

"Oh, yeah, I can see me telling James he won't do."

"I beg your pardon?" said a young woman who'd just come out of one of the stalls.

"Sorry, I was talking to myself." She rushed from the ladies' room, embarrassed by her foolishness.

No, she couldn't back out now. Besides, James was perfect for the role. And she didn't *really* have any interest in him. All the reasons for not choosing him for Daisy applied to Elise, too.

If she ever did consider marriage, it would be to a man who centered his world around her. Not the opposite. Actors were notoriously egotistical.

Which had been Richard's strong suit, too.

She reached the table, but she didn't bother to sit down. "Are you ready? I need to get home. I have some papers to grade."

"Sure. But I'm waiting for George to bring back my credit card."

Rather than just stand there like an idiot, she sat. "Okay."

George instantly appeared, and James signed the ticket.

She popped up like a jack-in-the-box as soon as he finished writing.

"You *are* in a hurry, aren't you," he said, frowning.

"I have an early class tomorrow." And a faulty resistance system for handsome men, apparently.

"Okay. So our next date—I mean, research meeting, should be Friday night, so you can sleep late the next morning."

"But today is Wednesday. We don't need to meet that often, do we?" she asked, hoping she was hiding her concern.

"Only if you want to convince your sisters. We still have a lot to learn about each other."

She supposed that was true. It seemed to her he'd spent most of his time talking to her friends, so she didn't think it was her fault they had to go out more often.

When they got in the car and he'd backed out into traffic, she said, "What's your favorite color?"

He looked at her, surprise on his face. Then, with a smile, he said, "Green."

She turned bright red since she was wearing green and he was staring at her sweater. "Oh. I didn't know."

"And yours?"

Her favorite color was green, too, but she didn't want to say that now. He'd think she was just saying that to agree with him.

"Red," she said firmly. "Red is my favorite color."

"I'm not surprised. It matches your cheeks," he pointed out, a grin on his lips.

She hoped he didn't remember Daisy's comment about her lies.

"Are you a morning person, or a night person?" she asked, hoping a change of subject would help her equilibrium.

"Do I have to be one or the other?"

That response startled her. "Isn't everyone?"

"I guess I'm more night than morning, but I don't like to sleep late. I don't need a lot of sleep."

"And I suppose you think people who do are lazy?"

He took his gaze off the road, frowning at her. "Are you trying to pick a fight with me?"

"No! I just— People who— Never mind." She crossed her arms over her chest and said nothing more.

They finished the drive in silence. Fortunately it wasn't a long drive.

After killing the motor, he partially turned toward her. "I take it you require a lot of sleep?"

"I need eight hours, like normal people."

"That means you're a night person, right? You stay up too late and then have trouble getting up. So we'll tell your sisters our being together works well because I can get you out of bed in the mornings," he said with a smile.

Elise stared at him in horror. "We'll do nothing of the sort!"

"Why? Surely you don't think they'll believe we're not sleeping with each other. We're not exactly teenagers."

"I suppose you think sex should be a part of dating?" She tried to keep her outrage under control.

"If there's no sexual attraction, there won't be an

engagement. If they're going to believe us, they have to think I can't keep my hands off you.''

"I'm not sure you're that good an actor," she snapped.

His chuckle surprised her, and she glared at him.

"Sweetheart, that part doesn't require any acting."

"What do you mean?"

"You're a beautiful woman. I'm a man. We men are drawn to beautiful women. And you look damn good in jeans."

"I don't— They're old."

"And fit you like a glove. It was a pure pleasure to follow you around tonight."

She wasn't sure she believed him, but she knew she'd be so self-conscious when she got out of the car, she'd scarcely be able to walk.

"Is sex all you ever think about?" she asked, hoping to stop this conversation.

"Nope. But it's nice to consider."

"There are other things more important. Like…" She thought desperately. "Like, are you a Republican or a Democrat?"

"You choose your men based on their political preferences?" he asked, incredulity in his voice.

"No! But it's something I should know."

"Okay. I'm neither. I vote based upon the candidate, not the political party." He smiled. "How about you?"

"Me? Uh, I'm—" What could she say? She did the same. "Me, too," she mumbled.

"What a relief. We can check that one off the list. What else?"

"Why do I have to come up with all the questions?

You should ask me about things that are important to you.'' Anything to get herself off the hook. Because her mind was a blank.

"Okay. Do you want children?"

She almost choked. She wouldn't have expected that question in a million years. "I said I wasn't interested in marriage!"

"That wasn't the question."

"Yes, it is. Because, like Daisy, I wouldn't choose to be a single parent. So that eliminates the prospect of children." She tried to keep any sadness out of her voice. The past few years, when she played with her nieces and nephews, a longing she tried to keep buried rose in her. But she'd accepted that she would never hold her own child in her arms.

"But what if someone in your family asks us about our plans to have children?"

"Well, to appease them, just say we want children but we don't know when or how many."

"Why are you so against marriage? Didn't your parents have a happy marriage?"

She definitely didn't like this line of questioning. "Yes, they did. I want to know your shoe size."

He blinked several times, drawing attention to his blue eyes. "My shoe size? Is there some psychological connection that I'm missing?"

She thought she'd pass out. Shoe size had been the first thing to come into her head, but women whispered about the shoe size being representative of the size of a certain other organ. Did James know that? She thought she'd die of embarrassment.

"I—I thought my sisters would expect me to know that."

"Well, for your sisters' edification, I wear a ten and a half. Oh, and I wear an extra-large shirt."

It was her turn to stare at him. Why would she need to know that?

"In case you're buying me a birthday present," he added, with a cheeky grin. "Actually, I thought you'd ask the more important question."

When he didn't continue, she asked, "What question?"

"Boxers or briefs?"

Elise tried to keep her chin up, fighting the embarrassment filling her, but she knew her cheeks gave her away. "Well?"

"Briefs. And you? Do you wear a thong?"

She'd stepped right into that one. Without warning, she opened the car door and got out. Then she leaned back in. "Never!" was her terse reply.

But he had the last word. Before she could slam the door, she heard him say in that deep, silky voice, "Too bad."

Chapter Four

"This is not going to work!" Elise assured her friends, pacing the floor.

After she'd reached her apartment, she'd called Phoebe and Daisy to come join her. She needed some reassurance.

"What's not going to work?" Daisy asked. "He's certainly handsome enough."

"Yes," Elise agreed with a sigh.

"Charm just oozes out of him," Phoebe added. "If he goes professional, he's going to be an enormous hit."

"Yes," Elise agreed again.

"So why won't he work?" Daisy asked, her gaze fixed on Elise.

"I'm the weak link. He makes me feel self-conscious. My sisters will never believe that I attracted that kind of man. It just won't work." She had to come up with some reason to break off the agreement. Even if she had to pay him the full amount. Even if she had to go to the wedding alone.

"Maybe his method acting will help." Phoebe's grin alerted Elise.

"Exactly what does that term mean?" James had mentioned it several times, but she really hadn't paid much attention. Phoebe's smile seemed to indicate it was important.

"Um, in general terms, you live the part, pretend it's really you."

"Live the part?" Elise asked, fear rising in her. The man was going to pretend he was *really* engaged to her? Oh, Lordy, she was in big trouble. If he touched her…kissed her— "I can't do it!"

Daisy was looking confused. "Why would method acting make you think you can't go through with it? I would think that would make it easier."

Elise couldn't answer.

Phoebe did. "I think Elise is afraid it will become too real for her. He might break her heart when it's over. That's why a lot of actors fall in love with their co-stars. They pretend to fall in love and, voilà, they are."

"Oh." Daisy shot a sympathetic look Elise's way.

"Yeah. And then, when it's over, a good method actor moves on to his next part. We amateurs aren't as skilled in—in moving on." Elise didn't think she would ever forget James Dillon, even now after one "research" evening. She wasn't falling in love. No, not that. But—but she could.

"I wish I could find someone like James," Daisy said with a sigh.

Elise saw a chance to break the agreement. "You're right. I've been too selfish. I'll tell James you have first dibs on any men we find and—"

"No! You heard him. He's not interested in being a father. And an actor really isn't a good prospect. I just mean someone who—a man who knows what he wants. A man who finds his own way in the world. I'm tired of men who are looking for a second mother.''

"He said he goes home to eat!" Elise protested, glad to find something to complain about.

"Daisy's right. He won't do for her. Besides, she's agreed to go out with the guy I found. Maybe he'll do the trick.'' Phoebe smiled at Daisy.

Daisy returned the smile, but Elise thought they both looked doubtful. "What's wrong with him?''

Both friends said, "Nothing!" at the same time.

"I mean, tell me about him. That's what I meant.''

Phoebe immediately launched into a sales campaign. "He's divorced, has a twelve-year-old daughter. That's how I met him. He brought his daughter to my class for young teenagers on how to apply makeup, so they don't look like a Las Vegas showgirl. And he's a dentist, very handsome.''

"He puts his hands in other people's mouths," Daisy muttered.

"He wears gloves, Daisy. And you haven't met him. He's charming.''

"As charming as James?" Daisy countered.

Phoebe made a face. "Not many men are as charming as James. But he's pleasant. Give him a chance.''

"Okay, okay. I said I'd go out with him. Friday, right?" Daisy asked.

"Right. When are you going to see James again?" Phoebe asked Elise.

"Friday.''

"Hmm. Guess I'm on my own Friday night.

Maybe I'll see if the Madisons will take pity on me,'' Phoebe said with a grin.

Elise smiled back. The elderly couple who lived just down the hall from Phoebe loved feeding their single neighbors. The three women had a standing invitation for dinner. The only cost was listening to stories of the Madisons' beloved grandson, Wyatt. Since none of them had ever met Wyatt, they had to take his besotted grandparents' word on how perfect he was.

''Maybe you should discuss Daisy with them. They'll immediately offer Wyatt as a solution, and our problems will be solved!'' Elise said with a chuckle.

''I don't think I could possibly be perfect enough for Wyatt,'' Daisy protested, laughing.

His perfection had become a standard joke among the three of them. When one of them intended to do something the other two thought was crazy, they always invoked Wyatt as a naysayer.

Phoebe looked pensive. ''You know, with all their talk about Wyatt, I don't even know what he does for a living. They're always talking about his childhood. Maybe because that's all they know. He certainly doesn't show up often. And they're such sweet people.''

They all nodded, but Elise's mind was focused on her own difficulties. Neither of her friends had shown her how she could get out of the situation she'd created.

In truth, she knew there wasn't a way out. Unless she was willing to go to Sharon's wedding alone.

And she wasn't. So she had to risk her heart to stay sane—only, risking her heart would drive her crazy.

What was a girl to do?

FOR THE NEXT two days, James chuckled often as he remembered the conversation he'd shared with Elise—and anticipated their Friday evening together.

"What's put you in such a happy mood?" MaryBelle asked as she served him breakfast Friday morning.

James immediately wiped away the smile. "Me? It's a beautiful day."

"We live in Phoenix, James. Most every day is beautiful, but that's never stopped you from acting like a grouchy bear."

"I'm not that bad, MaryBelle," he protested. But he was beginning to wonder. He'd gone back to the office yesterday and several people had commented on his change of attitude.

"It's a woman, isn't it?" MaryBelle suddenly guessed.

James immediately felt sympathy for Elise's blushes as his cheeks heated up. "I don't know what you're talking about."

"Aha! I was right. It's about time, too. It's unnatural for a handsome man like you to have nothing to do with women."

"Don't be silly, MaryBelle. I work with women all the time. Some of my best creative people are women."

"This is different," MaryBelle announced, a satisfied look on her round face. She picked up the coffeepot and poured him more. "Eat up, or I'll think you've lost your appetite because of this woman."

He glared at her.

"Ah, maybe she isn't as beautiful as she should be, if you're going to start growling again."

The temptation to assure his housekeeper that Elise was quite beautiful almost escaped his lips, until he caught the expectant look on her face. She was fishing for information. He pressed his lips together, then took a deep breath. "The coffee is especially good this morning, MaryBelle. New brand?"

"Nope. It just tastes better when you're in a good mood." After a moment, she asked, "Am I going to need to look for another job?"

Stunned, he put down his coffee cup. "What are you talking about? Have I upset you? You know I can't manage without you."

"I thought maybe with a new woman in the picture, she might not want me doin' the cooking."

Whether or not he gave her information about Elise, he couldn't let MaryBelle, sixty years young, worry about her future. She'd been a part of his life for almost ten years, and he couldn't ask for better. Rising, he hugged her rounded form. "I can't do without you, MaryBelle, new woman or not. Besides, she's a career woman. She'll love having you here."

"Aha! I knew there was someone!" MaryBelle crowed.

"You rat! You tricked me. You knew I'd worry about your hurt feelings. Shame on you!"

"It's your fault," MaryBelle proclaimed, her nose in the air. "You're too closemouthed for your own good."

He didn't agree with that, but he didn't mind letting MaryBelle know about Elise. He wanted to tell everyone about her, but that wasn't a good idea. Their being together was only temporary, he reminded himself. He headed for the door. "I won't be home for dinner tonight. Oh, and I'll need to borrow your car again."

"Okay. Thanks for the tune-up and wash, by the way. It drives a lot better now."

"I'll leave the keys to my car."

"No need. I'm not going anywhere."

With a wave, he was out the door, briefcase in hand, as usual. But he knew the smile on his lips was a new addition, as of two days ago.

SHE DIDN'T WEAR JEANS.

That smile insisted on spreading across James's mouth. He'd made her self-conscious. Tonight, she was dressed in a long-sleeved blouse and a skirt that fell to mid-calf. It wasn't tight enough to allow her shape to be seen, or full enough to swirl around her legs. And her blouse was done up all the way, except for the tiptop button.

She hadn't hidden her small waist, however. A belt with a silver buckle spanned her middle, like the bow on a present—and he was ready to start unwrapping. He found her demure outfit to be more enticing than any bikini.

"Shall we go?" she asked, staring at him.

"Not inviting me in tonight?" he asked, just to be ornery.

She'd met him at the door and had immediately

stepped forward and locked up behind her. He suspected she didn't trust him.

"I figured you were hungry."

"Starved," he assured her, letting his eyes tell her what kind of hunger he was talking about. She got the message. Her cheeks flamed again. He was almost ready to change his favorite color to rose, a beautiful dusty rose under peach-colored skin.

Instead of preceding him down the stairs, she suggested, "You go first."

He was about to grow concerned that he'd teased her too much.

Then she added, "It's my turn to enjoy the view."

"My pleasure, sweetheart," he assured her, grinning, and headed down. At the bottom, he turned to wait for her. "Okay?"

"Fine." She avoided looking at him.

They got in the car, but he didn't start the engine. "Just for the record, you're not a virgin, are you?"

"Why?"

"You seemed a little uncomfortable with our conversation Wednesday night. It occurred to me that you were less experienced than I expected."

She looked out the window rather than at him. "Just because I don't normally discuss sex with men doesn't mean I've never— No, I'm not a virgin."

"Good." He started the engine and backed out. "I've chosen another restaurant this evening. I hope you like Italian?"

"Yes, I love it."

Okay, so he'd made the right choice. She'd be more relaxed, and he'd learn even more delightful facts about Dr. Elise Foster. It was so hard to picture her as a college professor.

"Do you like teaching at ASU?"

She looked surprised. "I love it. I love the French language. It's beautiful, lyrical, and I love sharing it with others."

"I bet your students love the language, too, when you're finished with them."

"You make it sound like I force-feed them."

"No, I suspect you seduce them," he said softly, imagining listening to her for an hour, a smile on his lips.

"What? What do you mean?"

"Sorry, just a phrase. Listening to your voice is such a pleasure, I think you could convince me of anything."

"I didn't mean to overreact, but in this day and age, we have to be very careful." She folded her hands in her lap.

"Maybe I should've found a French restaurant and let you order for us," he suggested.

She rolled her eyes. "Why? You speak Arizonan as well as I do. You don't really think the waiter would be French, do you?"

"Surely there are some Frenchmen in Phoenix."

"There are, but they're usually the chef, not the waiters. I've had several come speak to my classes."

"Do you cook French dishes?"

He was surprised by the suspicion that filled her gaze.

"Why? Are you hoping I'll cook for you instead of your mom? Or cook a meal for you to impress someone?"

The tension in her voice confused him. "I was just making conversation, Elise, trying to get to know you. What did I do wrong?"

She looked away. "I'm sorry."

"That doesn't explain the problem. What is it?"

"M-my fiancé didn't want me to have a career unless it was entertaining his clients. The only schooling he wanted me to bother with was Cordon Bleu 101 so he could impress them."

"I hope you kicked him out on his behind."

"My family didn't have that reaction."

"Well, they should've. You weren't hiring on to be his housekeeper. You were going to be his wife. Didn't he care about what *you* wanted?" He thought the guy sounded like a jerk.

They'd reached the restaurant, and he parked. Then he turned to look at Elise. She hadn't responded to his statement. "Elise? Did I hurt your feelings? Are you all right?"

She blinked rapidly before looking at him, but he could still see the tears pooled in her eyes. "James, don't be—be so charming, please. I can't—"

"What are you talking about?"

"No man has ever— Even my family thought I was crazy because I objected to Richard's agenda."

"What did your brother say?"

"Chance? Oh, he didn't say much. He tried to stay uninvolved in what he called 'emotional girl stuff.'"

"That was probably smart," James agreed with a chuckle, "but it would've been better if he'd supported you."

She shrugged her shoulders. "This looks like a nice restaurant."

Clearly she was ready to change the subject. "I haven't tried it before, but it came highly recommended."

Once they were seated inside, he decided he'd made the right choice. Each booth had high backs and swinging saloon doors, giving them the illusion they were in a small room all alone. "Guess no one will interrupt us here," he said with a smile.

"I hope at least the waiter stops by, or we'll starve to death," Elise returned, smiling now too.

James was relieved. He didn't want her unhappy, but he felt as if he'd uncovered a lot in the short drive. When he combined the information about her fiancé and her taking care of her six sisters, it was easy to understand her resistance to marriage.

A thought suddenly struck him. "Richard is the only man you've slept with, isn't he."

The waiter opened the swinging door. "Good evening, I'm your waiter for the evening. Richard is my name."

Elise turned a bright red.

ELISE LET JAMES do the ordering. Since he consulted her on her preferences, he actually asked the waiter for exactly what she would have ordered. Richard used to order his own choices and expect her to like them.

She'd been an idiot ever to put up with the man.

The amazing thing was James's agreement. She hadn't expected him to even understand her problem with Richard's attitude, much less support her. She'd told Phoebe and Daisy about Richard's controlling nature, of course, in one of their late-night chats, and hadn't been surprised when they'd agreed with her assessment of him. They were women.

The waiter finally left the table, and James leaned back against the booth. ''I'm right, aren't I?''

''Yes, thank you. You ordered exactly what I wanted.''

''That's not what I meant. You've only slept with Richard, haven't you.''

''James! You have no right to ask such personal questions! I haven't asked that of you.''

''What do you want to know?'' he asked, spreading his hands wide.

''I don't see any need to discuss our past lives. My sisters won't ask questions about your past.''

''Then they're mighty unusual women.''

''If they do, I'll tell them it's none of their business, nor mine, either, for that matter.''

He leaned forward, and even with the table between them she found herself pressing against the back of the booth.

''You're telling me even if we were really engaged, you wouldn't ask about my past partners? You wouldn't even want to know about my ex-wife?''

Shocked out of her self-consciousness, she leaned forward. ''You've been married? You must've been very young.''

For the first time in a while, he was the one to seem ill-at-ease. ''Yeah.'' He busied himself with his napkin.

''See? It's uncomfortable to be grilled by a stranger,'' she pointed out.

''I wasn't grilling you!'' he snapped. ''It seemed

to me you haven't spent a lot of time with men, but if you were a virgin, I—''

"I'm not. We've established that. And I told you I hadn't dated much. So, we can move on." She certainly hoped they would. She was tired of turning a bright red every time she talked to this man.

Silence followed. Okay, so they didn't have anything in common. Well, they had the school. She'd talk about school. "How was your day? What play are you working on now?"

He didn't look enthusiastic. "Um, Shakespeare. We're doing a Shakespeare play."

"Oh, really. I thought you were going to skip him this year since you just did a Molière. I heard you were going for contemporary comedies to tempt a younger crowd." She stared at him curiously. There had been a big debate on campus, the classics versus the popular.

"Oh, you mean our production. Right, of course. I thought you were referring to my classes. We're working on Shakespeare in class, but our—our public presentation is a contemporary."

"Which one?"

He looked a little lost, and she stared at him.

"I believe it's a Neil Simon. Yes, a Neil Simon. He's a very good writer, you know."

Her lips twitched. Did he think she was an idiot? "Yes, I heard," she said smoothly.

Now he blushed bright red. She loved turning the tables on him.

"Of course you have. I didn't mean to imply— I was embarrassed because I couldn't think of the name of it."

"It's not a test, James," she assured him kindly. "I thought you would be involved in it, that's all."

"Not yet. I've had too much to do for my classes."

"How many hours do you teach each week?"

He more easily fielded that question. "Nine."

"And you also take classes? That's a heavy load. Are you sure you have time for—for our nonsense?"

"It's not nonsense," he assured her, more confident now. "I'm calling it our Campaign for Elise's Sanity."

She chuckled. "Short and to the point. And very accurate." She sighed. "I haven't said anything to my family yet. I wanted to be sure— I mean, you might've changed your mind, so—"

"I'm not going to change my mind. I'm enjoying myself. And I hope you are, too."

She blushed again. Oh, yes, she was enjoying herself, part of the time—the part where she wasn't horribly embarrassed. And James had improved her dream time dramatically. "Yes, it's—it's been interesting."

He chuckled. "People are saying my attitude has improved."

"Your attitude?"

"Sometimes I can be a little grouchy."

She could believe that. When he'd criticized Richard, his expression had been firm, determined, strong. Not that she was complaining. But she could imagine he'd be a formidable foe.

"And—and I changed that?" she asked, doubtful.

"Oh, yes. Just thinking about our conversation Wednesday night put a smile on my face."

She was grateful when the doors swung open again and the waiter put the glass of tea she'd ordered in front of her. Maybe the cold drink would cool the heat in her cheeks.

Chapter Five

By the time dinner was over, James thought Elise was more at ease with him. They'd had a lively discussion on their favorite authors. Once they finished eating, Elise led the conversation to television. For *him,* she added, a wicked smile on her lips.

He turned it into a discussion of their favorite advertising spots on television. He was pleased when she named as her favorite one of the campaigns he'd written.

"Of course, it's my favorite," she exclaimed. "I love commercials that make me laugh—and when the man sits down on the loaf of bread by mistake, it always cracks me up."

"Yeah. Me, too. What do you think about this ad that's an ongoing saga, with a romance in it?"

"Oh, you mean the one for the steak restaurant? I'm enjoying it. It's an ad I actually look forward to. Have they started a new chapter yet?"

"Not until next week," he assured her, smiling back.

"How do you know that?"

Uh-oh. "I read it in the Business section of the newspaper."

"I missed it."

"You read the newspaper every day?" he asked. He'd always thought college professors hardly knew there was a world out there, their lives were so isolated.

"Of course. I particularly check the Business section because I like to know what industries are in the area that would be interested in bilingual employees. That's one of the ways I show my students that French is still relevant."

"It would be easier if you taught Spanish, as close to the border as we are," he pointed out.

"I know." She propped up her chin, a somewhat discouraged look on her face. "Enrollment is a battle we fight every day. The past year or two we've even picked up our numbers, but it's a concern every semester."

"Numbers are important," he said gravely, thinking of his own concerns about the number of people responding to the ads he'd created.

"I'll admit, at this age the boys are more interested in the topless beaches in France than they are in the job prospects, but I hope they'll remember what I say later."

"You mean you admit that males are sometimes interested in sex?" he teased, referring to their conversation on Wednesday night.

"I think 'sometimes' might be an understatement."

"Yeah, probably. By the way, have I mentioned how nice you look tonight?"

She shook her head.

"Well, you do. Maybe even better than in the jeans," he added, grinning.

"You're just trying to embarrass me," she told him, sitting straighter on the bench seat, like a prim and proper teacher. "But I'm not going to blush, so you might as well give up."

Since he'd already decided they needed a little more method acting, he planned on causing her to blush a lot before they ended the evening. But he didn't mention that fact now.

"Yes, ma'am."

The waiter interrupted them with the bill. James had his credit card ready and handed it to him, and the waiter disappeared.

"You are keeping track of your expenses, aren't you?" Elise asked, frowning.

"Stop worrying. I know how to keep an expense account," he assured her carelessly.

"You do? I didn't think actors had expense accounts."

"Uh, it was for a summer job I had once."

"A summer job? I gather you weren't selling fries at a burger shop." Her tone indicated her doubt.

"Nope. I was working for my dad. He wanted to teach me about the big, bad world." He actually had worked for his father a few summers, doing yard work and repairs to the house.

"Is your father alive?"

"Yeah, he and Mom live in Tucson. He plays a lot of golf now, but he used to run a manufacturing plant down there."

The waiter returned, and James was glad. He'd

have to be more careful when he answered Elise's questions or she'd figure out something was wrong.

He escorted her to the car, which pleased him. Not because he was ready for the evening to end. No, not that. He was looking forward to the next part of their research. All evening, he'd stared at those soft lips. And as soon as they got back to her apartment, he was going to taste them.

ELISE WAS FEELING better about their agreement. She'd managed an entire evening without falling apart. And once they'd started talking about general things, rather than her love life, she hadn't blushed once.

He was still charming, of course. It seemed to be a natural thing with him. But with a table between them, she could manage just fine.

In the car, as he drove, she asked him if he preferred acting in a comedy or a drama. That question launched a discussion of their favorite movies. Amazingly, she discovered they liked a lot of the same ones. Of course, he preferred a few bang-bang shoot-'em-ups, mostly contemporary, that she'd never seen, and he hadn't bothered with *Sense and Sensibility* or *Emma*.

"So next time shall we take in a movie? How about Sunday evening?" he suggested as he parked the car in front of her place.

"Monday, Wednesday and Friday are my early classes," she pointed out.

"Okay, we'll make it Monday night. What time's your first class on Tuesday?"

"Eleven, but I keep office hours from nine-thirty until class."

"Nine-thirty? Unfair, I have to be at work at eight o'clock," he teased.

She stared at him. "I didn't know the Drama Department scheduled any classes that early. I'm surprised."

"It's not classes," he said hurriedly. "I do some prep work for my supervising professor."

"Oh, I guess that's not too bad. Well, thanks for a lovely evening," she began as she reached for the door handle.

"Wait."

"Yes? Did I forget something?"

"Yeah, I think you did. This—"

As his head drew closer, she suddenly realized what he meant. She had every intention of protesting, but somehow she didn't get the words out until it was too late.

His warm, sexy lips covered hers, lured hers into clinging to his, opening to his, inviting him in, even though she'd had no intention of doing so.

He accepted the invitation.

His hands did even more, encircling her, pulling her across the bench seat, pressing her against his long, lean form. He lifted his mouth and quickly reslanted it on hers to take the kiss deeper. Somehow, her arms ended up around his neck.

She thought she'd never been kissed like that before. A startling realization for a woman of her age.

"What was that?" she muttered, staring fiercely into his blue eyes when he lifted his head.

"Sweetheart, if you don't know, I definitely need

to practice more,'' he whispered, even as he lowered his head again.

The second kiss was even better than the first…and frightened Elise. The evening had gone so well. She'd thought she could handle the situation. Now he was proving she couldn't.

"Stop!" she urged, jerking her lips from his, even as her body protested.

"Why? We're doing so well," he murmured, and started to kiss her again.

"No!" She took a deep breath, trying to suppress the hysterical note in her voice. "We don't need to practice. We're both able to— I mean, we're experienced. This isn't necessary."

"You want me to stop?"

She stared at him. Hadn't he been listening? "Yes, that's what I said."

"Then why are your arms still around my neck?"

She jerked them back as if someone had poured boiling water on them. "I didn't realize— I forgot."

He gave her a cocky grin. "Anytime you want to forget again, just let me know, Elise. I'll be happy to accommodate you."

"Thank you, but that won't be necessary," she assured him, looking away after taking one last quick glance at his lips. Hard to believe a kiss had brought that much pleasure.

She reached for the door handle again, determined to get out of the car before she changed her mind. *Temptation, thy name is James.*

He didn't try to stop her. He got out, too, and came around to meet her at the front of the car. "I'll walk you to the door," he said in a husky voice.

"No, it's perfectly safe. Well-lit. I—I'll be all right."

"I'm walking you to the door," he insisted, taking hold of her arm.

Shivers ran over her body at his touch. Since he had an obstinate look on his face, she decided it would be quicker if she let him accompany her. Then he'd go away.

"Why are you in such a hurry?" he asked, as they rushed up the stairs.

"It—it might rain," she suggested.

"In Phoenix? Maybe in July, Elise, but it doesn't rain much the rest of the year."

"I thought I saw some clouds," she argued.

She came to a halt in front of her door, frantically searching for her keys. He stood patiently beside her, waiting, which surprised her. Maybe she was worrying about nothing. He probably had no interest in kissing her again. She was being foolish.

Drawing a sigh of relief both at finding her keys and deciding she'd been wrong about James, she smiled at him. "I found them."

"Good," he said, and swept her back into his arms for another devastating kiss.

"HEY, BRO, you got a minute?" Bobby asked, when James answered the phone the next morning.

James sat up in bed and searched for the alarm clock he kept by his bed. It was almost ten o'clock. He hadn't slept that late in years.

"Uh, yeah, Bobby, what is it?" Then it occurred to him that his brother might have heard rumors about him and Elise. He clutched the phone more tightly.

"You remember the girl who wasn't projecting?"

James couldn't even think of a proper response. That question had come out of left field as far as he was concerned.

"Hey, James, did I wake you up?"

"Yeah, but that's all right, I—"

"Man, you never used to sleep late. Is something wrong?"

"No, not at all. I had a late night. Now what about that girl?"

"Sandy. Remember? She wasn't projecting and—"

"Yeah, I remember. What's wrong? Did I hurt her feelings?" He couldn't think of any other reason Bobby would want him to remember the girl.

"No, of course not. I told her the same thing. But her dad's a bigwig with one of the banks in town, and Sandy's invited me to a party they're having honoring her dad. I don't want to embarrass her by driving up in my old car. I wondered if I could borrow yours."

"Sure."

"That was quick. You haven't even asked what day," Bobby pointed out.

"Doesn't matter. I—I can always borrow MaryBelle's car if I need it. Or rent one."

Bobby chuckled. "Yeah, right, I can just see you behind the wheel of MaryBelle's car."

James didn't want to discuss the likelihood of that happening. "When do you need it?"

"Uh, tonight. I should've called earlier, but I was debating with myself."

"You know I don't mind. I offered to buy you a car when your last one broke down."

"I know you did. You're a great brother, but I have to make it on my own."

"You're a pretty special brother yourself. Be careful about dating someone who isn't satisfied with you and what you have." That described Sylvia to a tee. James wouldn't want that for anyone, much less his baby brother.

"You taught me that lesson, bro. How is old Sylvia?"

"Getting older." James laughed. "I don't really know, Bobby. I try to avoid seeing her as much as possible." The meetings happened more than he liked. Her current husband was with one of James's client companies.

"Well, if you don't mind, Sandy will drop me by your house in a few minutes and I'll borrow your Mercedes...if you're sure you don't mind."

"I don't mind at all. I'll be here."

He hung up the phone and sank down onto the pillow again. How ironic. He wasn't driving his Mercedes because of a woman—but his brother was, for the same reason.

But Elise was well worth giving up the powerful machine. For a while. The kisses they'd shared last night had told him that. He'd thought he was in love with Sylvia when they'd married. But her kisses didn't compare to Elise's. None of the women who'd eagerly offered their lips to him even came close to Elise.

Not that he was in love with her. He just…enjoyed her. In so many ways. Getting to know Elise had become the most fascinating project he'd ever undertaken.

His body thought so, too. He'd gotten home by ten o'clock, not exactly a late Friday night. But it had taken three or four hours to settle down, to convince his body nothing was going to happen.

The thought of her, the lingering scent of her on his fingertips, the remembrance of their kisses, had made it impossible to sleep until late into the night.

He rubbed his eyes. Damn, he needed some coffee.

He rolled out of bed and tugged on a pair of jeans, grabbed a T-shirt from a drawer and headed down the stairs while he pulled it over his head.

MaryBelle didn't really work on the weekends unless he had something in particular he needed her to do, but she lived in her own apartment in the house, so she always made coffee, and, if he wanted it, breakfast.

This morning he wanted it.

She was sitting at the table doing the crossword puzzle. "Morning, Sleeping Beauty."

"Coffee," he growled, heading straight for the coffeepot on the kitchen cabinet.

MaryBelle got to her feet. "I'll fix you some breakfast. I have pancake batter all ready."

Having poured his coffee, he stopped to kiss her cheek before he sat down at the kitchen table. "Thanks."

"Want bacon with the pancakes?"

"Yes, please," he said, and reached for the newspaper.

"Don't get my crossword," she warned.

His only response was a grunt because he was already immersed in the headlines. At least they took his mind off Elise and when he'd see her again.

ELISE MET HER FRIENDS at the pool.

Almost all the residents of Mesa Blue spent weekends gathered around the huge pool. Not only did it alleviate the heat, but even in the late winter it was a soothing place to relax. Even Daisy, who usually worked Saturdays, had taken today off.

"Well, who wants to start?" Phoebe asked as she rubbed sunscreen on her fair skin.

Elise knew Phoebe was asking for a report of their Friday nights and she wanted to get it over with. She'd already prepared in her mind what she would tell her friends. "I will. Everything went well. We have similar tastes in movies and television ads, and—"

"Television ads?" Daisy asked as she plopped her big straw hat on her head. She hated to freckle.

Elise shrugged her shoulders. "Yes. Somehow we discussed ads on television. Anyway, we got along fine. And we ate at a very nice Italian restaurant. Your turn, Daisy."

The other two stared at her.

Phoebe finally said, "Are we on a schedule?"

"Why, no, what do you mean?" Elise asked, keeping her eyes closed behind her sunshades.

"She means you ran through your description of the evening like a news reporter only allotted thirty seconds to tell her story," Daisy said, sitting up on her chaise longue. "Did something happen you're not telling us?"

"What could happen? We were just getting to know each other. Conversation, that's all," she assured them. Her mouth was dry. Lying seemed to be hard work. Especially lying and not blushing.

"Hmm, okay," Phoebe said reluctantly. "Your turn, Daisy."

"Well, I can be even briefer than Elise. No way, José. Your turn, Phoebe."

"Now, come on, Daisy, he's a nice man," Phoebe protested.

"Yes, he is, especially if you want to hear about the new X-ray machine he bought for his office. And how much his Mercedes cost him. Did I mention how many new clients he's gotten this past year? Or where he spent his last vacation? Then there's his Rolex. I even got to listen to it tick," she assured them, pretending excitement.

Phoebe held up her hand. "Okay, enough said. Sorry."

Daisy immediately looked contrite. "You tried, Phoebe. It's not your fault it didn't work out."

"He wasn't like that when I met him," Phoebe assured her.

"I probably brought out the worst in him," Daisy said with a sigh.

Knowing Daisy didn't want any more questions, Elise said, "How about you, Phoebe? Did you eat with the Madisons?"

"I did. We had a great dinner. And talked about…" she paused, looking at them expectantly.

Together Elise and Daisy said, "Wyatt."

Phoebe chuckled. "Right. I asked them why he didn't visit them more, but they defended him, of course. Said he couldn't get away right now. He was very busy, and very successful—perfect as usual."

"Did you ask them what keeps him busy?" Daisy asked.

"I was going to, but then dear, sweet Rolland asked me how I did on that test I had in Chemistry, and I got distracted. Aren't they the dearest people?"

Daisy and Elise exchanged a look. They'd talked before about how good the Madisons were for Phoebe. She didn't have much of a relationship with her own mother, who didn't live nearby. The Madisons kind of filled that role for their friend.

"Yes, they are," Elise agreed. "And Helen is such a good cook."

"Yes, she is," Phoebe said, patting her flat stomach. "I don't think I can eat all day long just to make up for last night."

"I don't see any problem, sweetcheeks," Jeff Hawkin crooned in Phoebe's ear, startling her. He stood and leaned on the long netted pole he used to clean debris from the pool.

"Oh, Jeff, I didn't hear you come up," she said with a gasp, putting her hand to her chest.

"I was quiet because I was admiring all the natural beauty around the pool," he said, and bowed deeply in their direction.

"Dear Jeff," Daisy said, fanning herself with her straw hat. "If only you were ten years older."

"I keep telling you, Daisy, I'm old enough."

Elise couldn't keep a smile from her face. Jeff flirted outrageously with every woman in the complex, even Helen Madison who was old enough to be his great-grandmother.

Jeff turned to Elise. ''And you, young lady, I heard you've been stepping out on me. Who's this guy who's coming around? I haven't checked him out yet.

''Feel free to check now,'' a deep, silky voice said from behind Elise.

Chapter Six

Elise almost fell off her chaise longue. "James!" she shrieked. "What—what are you doing here?"

That left eyebrow went up. "Enjoying the view?" he suggested, grinning at all three ladies.

"You got that right, man," Jeff agreed, returning James's grin.

Elise reached for the cover-up she'd brought down. Which was ridiculous. Her one-piece suit was modest compared to most women's. But with James staring at her, she felt naked.

Jeff stepped forward, his hand extended. "Jeff Hawkin, pool cleaner and handyman extraordinaire."

"James Dillon," James offered, shaking his hand.

"Pull up a seat and join us," Jeff invited.

Elise felt like objecting. No one asked her about James staying, and he was her guest. At least she thought he was. Maybe she'd been right Wednesday night and he was attracted to one of her friends.

While she was thinking, he'd been accepting Jeff's invitation. When his warm hand slid along her calf to shift her legs so he could sit on the end of the chaise longue, she jumped again.

"You don't mind if I borrow this spot, do you, Elise?" he asked after he'd sat down.

"It would be a little late if I did," she pointed out.

"Of course, she doesn't," Phoebe said. "Were you in the neighborhood, James, or do you live near here?"

"I live closer to the school," he said.

It occurred to Elise that she'd never bothered to ask where he lived. He probably didn't mind. Starving artists weren't house proud, usually.

"This is a great pool," James said, looking around.

"Yeah, it's the best. It's even heated in the winter months. The air temperature's okay for swimming in winter, but sometimes pool water's too cold to be comfortable. But not our pool," Jeff boasted proudly. "Did you bring your trunks with you?"

"Why, no, I didn't. I didn't think about swimming. I just thought I'd see what Elise had planned for the day." He turned to send Elise that warm, sexy smile of his, and all her objections to his unannounced visit dissolved.

"I've got a clean extra pair. Why don't you borrow them? Maybe we can get up a game of volleyball. How about it, girls? Will you play?"

Jeff frequently acted like a social director on a cruise ship, but everyone enjoyed his antics. Elise nodded, as did Daisy and Phoebe.

"Are you sure we have enough people?" Phoebe asked.

"I'll round up some more. Come on, James, I'll show you where to change. Rest up, ladies, while we're gone. You'll need your energy when we get back.''

James, for the first time, showed a hint of hesitation, and looked at Elise.

She nodded with a smile. It wasn't an elaborate invitation, but his smile widened and he jumped up and followed Jeff.

''Well, that was interesting,'' Phoebe said, watching the two men walk away.

''What do you mean?'' Elise asked.

''You were with him last night and he's already back for more. And you two communicate pretty well without words.''

Daisy nodded. ''Yeah, you can kind of feel a tension in the air when they're together. I noticed it Wednesday night.''

''Don't be silly. You know I'm—'' she broke off and looked around to be sure she wouldn't be overheard ''—paying him. You're imagining things.''

Her friends looked at each other and nodded. But Elise was afraid they weren't agreeing with her.

Phoebe said, ''I hadn't intended to do anything energetic, but after that meal last night, I suppose it would be a good idea. Helen had made a cheesecake with strawberry topping to die for.''

''Ooh,'' Daisy said softly. ''I love those home-made cheesecakes of hers.''

''Maybe if we dropped by this afternoon for a visit, she'd serve it,'' Phoebe said. ''And they can rave some more about Wyatt. You know they always love that.''

''Sounds like cupboard love to me,'' Elise teased.

Daisy just nodded, but Phoebe protested, ''You

know we all love them. They're such wonderful people.'' She paused, then said, ''You know, did it ever occur to either of you that Wyatt might really *be* perfect? With grandparents like Rolland and Helen, it might be possible.''

Shifting to her side, Daisy looked at Phoebe. ''But no one wants a perfect man. Maybe that's why dear Wyatt hasn't married. He's too good to be true.''

''Doubtful,'' Elise assured her friend. ''But since the dentist was a washout, we've got to find someone else for you. Hey, have we asked Jeff if he knows anyone? The book says talk to neighbors.''

''I want someone old enough to stay out past ten o'clock. Jeff's too young,'' Daisy protested.

''But he may know someone older. After all, he bartends down at The Prickly Pear part time,'' Phoebe pointed out.

''Just what I need. A barfly.''

''*We* hang out there, too,'' Elise pointed out.

Daisy shrugged.

Before they could continue their conversation, Jeff and his recruits emerged from the building.

''Hey, he got Frannie, Bill and Rolland,'' Daisy said, a speculative look in her eye. ''I wonder how Frannie arranged that?''

''I don't know, but good for her,'' Elise said. Frannie Fitzgerald was a delightful neighbor, even if she dressed a little on the colorful side. And she loved anything with cats on it. Today, she wore a skirted suit, black with the outline of cats all over it.

Bill White was the building superintendent. He and Frannie were about the same age, and she had a terrible crush on him, though she pretended she didn't. He seemed to ignore her.

"Maybe we should loan her our book," Daisy whispered.

"You think Frannie isn't self-confident?" Phoebe asked with a laugh.

"I don't know, but she hasn't caught his interest yet."

Elise wasn't so sure. Bill was walking behind Frannie and Jeff, and she thought of James's words about following her around. Bill's gaze was on Frannie.

James was walking between Bill and Rolland Madison, seemingly involved in conversation with both men. Rolland was in his eighties, but in magnificent shape. He'd served in the Navy for many years and his posture still showed it.

"Have I got a deal for you!" Jeff assured them as he reached poolside. "I couldn't talk Helen into joining us, but to make up for it, she said she'd have lunch ready for everyone when we finished."

Phoebe cheered, but all four ladies, including Frannie, protested Helen doing all that work.

"Now, girls, you know she worries about you not eating properly," Rolland said. "She'll love it. She'd rather cook all day long than play volleyball in the pool."

"Come on, James, help me put up the net," Jeff called just before he stepped off the edge into the pool, splashing all of them. Though the water was warm, they all yelled, anyway, knowing Jeff expected some reaction.

James laughed and started to move to the pool, but

first he ducked down and kissed Elise. Startled, she had no time to react before he, too, jumped in.

Rolland looked at her. "Your young man seems very nice, Elise. Helen was delighted to meet him."

"Oh, Rolland, he's not—I mean, I just met him on Wednesday."

Rolland stared into space. "Sometimes it doesn't take long. You know Helen and I only knew each other a week before we got married, and it's been sixty-eight glorious years."

The couple loved to talk about their brief courtship, so they'd all heard the story, but it moved Elise to tears every time. "I know, but there aren't all that many men around as wonderful as you, Rolland."

He cocked an eyebrow, similar to James, and said, "Well, now, that could be true," shooting them a grin that was too cute.

Phoebe stood and gave him a hug. "Helen had better keep her eye on you, young man."

"Come on in, everyone," Jeff called.

Frannie, who'd been surprisingly quiet since she'd arrived, asked, "How do we choose up teams?"

"James and I took care of that," Jeff assured her. "You and Bill are going to be on his team with Elise. The rest of us will skunk you!"

"Okay, as long as I don't get my hair wet. Remember, you promised." She moved around the pool to the wide steps and practically tiptoed into the water.

Her hair, bright red, always made Elise think of Lucille Ball. Frannie had hers pinned up in an elaborate beehive style, as usual.

Daisy leaned toward Elise as they got up. "Do you think she believed Jeff when he promised that?"

"No," Elise responded. "But she'd shave her head if it got Bill's attention."

They joined the others with grins on their faces.

Several hours later, Frannie's hair wasn't the only thing that was wet—so was everyone in the game as well as a number of observers around the pool. The game had been a rousing success. Elise had even grown comfortable around James in her swimsuit—until he touched her. When he spanned her waist with his big hands and lifted her above the net to spike the ball, she fell back into his arms and they both sank.

His lips found hers before she got back to the top of the water.

Jeff had protested his assist, but Elise was too dazed to answer. Bill, much to everyone's surprise, pointed out it wasn't forbidden in the rules. He even went so far as to lift Frannie to hit the next ball. She was so startled, the ball sailed past her out of the pool. Which, of course, was good for the other team.

Now, after having taken down the net, they were all lolling in the water, too tired to think of climbing out. Helen appeared, however, warning them that lunch would be ready in fifteen minutes.

The women all began scrambling for the side of the pool. Fifteen minutes wasn't much time to recover from pool volleyball.

"Elise?"

She turned around to find James coming toward her. "Yes?"

"I'll head on home. I didn't mean to barge in."

Rolland, just behind him, immediately protested. "Helen is counting on you joining us."

"But Elise didn't even know I was coming—"

"Please, James, stay and have lunch with us," Elise asked. "Helen really would be offended if you left. You'll love her."

"If you're sure," he said again, giving her plenty of opportunity to send him away.

"I'm sure."

"Me, too," Rolland added.

Jeff splashed by. "Come on, James, I'll race you to the shower. Man, you've got a wicked serve."

And like two little boys, the men were racing across the sidewalk to Jeff's apartment.

Rolland smiled at them. "Nice to see such good manners and boyish charm. Good combination. Reminds me of our Wyatt," he said, nodding to Elise.

"Yes, I suppose it does," she agreed with a smile.

So there were two perfect men. Who would have thought it?

JAMES DECIDED Helen should open her own restaurant. No New Age cuisine for her. She made great food that filled a man up. He wouldn't dare tell MaryBelle what a great lunch he'd had.

It had to be good for a man: Rolland was living proof. In his eighties, and he looked and moved as well as Bill, who was no slouch himself, even though James figured he was around fifty.

James couldn't remember when he'd had such an entertaining day. And on top of that, he'd gotten to spend it with Elise. He hadn't been able to resist the urge to drop in on her to see what she was doing. It worried him, his need to see her, but he decided it was curiosity and would fade after a while.

She'd slipped on a pale green wraparound dress, big white gardenias painted on the material. The tie that appeared to hold the dress together tempted him beyond belief. The only thing needed to make the day perfect was a big bed, Elise and him. Alone.

"James? You gone to sleep?" Bill asked.

"No! I was just thinking about—things," James said.

Bill's knowing grin told James he understood. James noted how his gaze traveled across the room to Frannie, who was helping the women clear the table. Maybe he understood for a good reason.

"I hope you don't mind," Jeff said, leaning toward James.

"What do you mean?"

"Well, Helen loves to play Trivial Pursuit. We like to indulge her."

"After eating a meal like that, Trivial Pursuit sounds perfect. As long as I don't look too dumb. Do we have any ringers in here?"

"Frannie's pretty good," Bill said.

"We'll probably need to play partners," James said, grinning at Bill. "Just claim her now, and you'll have the advantage."

Bill turned beet red. "Oh, I couldn't—"

"Sure you could," Jeff urged. He stood up. "I'll get the Trivial Pursuit, Helen. Phoebe, you want to read the questions?"

"Yes, please," Phoebe called from the kitchen.

"Okay, we're going to partner up. Daisy, you'll be my partner," Jeff said, organizing everything.

"Elise will be James's, Rolland and Helen will be together, and Frannie and Bill."

James had never thought of Trivial Pursuit as a sexy game, but he and Elise sat close together on the floor around the coffee table. Every time they had a question, he slid his arm around her and whispered in her ear.

Sometimes, if he was lucky, she'd turn to face him and he'd snatch a quick kiss. She protested, trying not to be obvious to the others who pretended not to watch them, but James shushed her. He told her she was holding up the game.

By the time the game ended several hours later, he was in such a constant state of arousal, it was becoming painful. He only hoped it wasn't obvious to everyone.

Jeff, as if reluctant to have the afternoon end, suggested they all go to The Prickly Pear, since he was on duty that night. James was afraid he couldn't bear much more togetherness with Elise without doing something about how much he wanted her.

"I think I'd better go, Jeff, but thanks for the invite. And for the day. It's been a lot of fun." He stood up and crossed to Helen. "Mrs. Madison, that was an incredible meal. Thank you so much for inviting me."

"Anytime, James, dear. Elise's friends are always welcome. And please, call me Helen."

He thanked her again, calling her Helen. Then he shook Bill's and Rolland's hands, said goodbye to all the women. Elise was standing by the door, and he grabbed her hand and tugged her after him. "I need a word with Elise, but thanks again."

He closed the door behind them.

"What did you need to say?"

"This—" He pulled her against him and kissed her deeply, pressing her to his body. He didn't know how long they kissed, but it wasn't long enough. However, the sound of the door opening broke them apart. Elise stared at him, her green eyes wide. He dropped another kiss on her lips and hurried away, just as her friends came out of the Madisons' condo.

WHEN JAMES CAME DOWN to breakfast the next morning, MaryBelle was again at the table.

"Made muffins yesterday. That's all you get for breakfast this morning, except for the sausage I just cooked. And juice and coffee, of course."

He smiled. "Who could complain about that?"

"You, on some days. But since you found this woman, you've quit complaining. I assume that's where you disappeared to, yesterday. Have a nice day?"

"How do you know I wasn't at work all day?"

"Because they called looking for you."

He frowned. "But you didn't leave me a message."

"They said not to. Figured if you were having a good time, you wouldn't want to be bothered."

He shrugged his shoulders. Before, he might have worried until he found out what the problem was. This morning, he decided it could wait.

"Looks like your brother found a girlfriend, too."

"Bobby? You mean because he borrowed my car last night?" He picked up the cup of coffee MaryBelle had given him while they chatted.

She carried over a plate of muffins and sausage and set it in front of him. "Nope. Because his picture is in the paper."

The implications of that occurrence took a minute to sift through James's contentment. Then he set his coffee down with a thud, spilling some over the side.

"What? Where?"

MaryBelle tisked as she got up to get a cloth to wipe the table.

"MaryBelle, where's the picture?" he demanded.

"I folded it and left it there by your plate," she said calmly, before sitting down again. "She's pretty."

James grabbed the paper and opened it. The society column was filled with photos of couples posing for pictures. Several of them were couples dancing, one at a private birthday party for a local politician. But there were several pictures taken at the dinner honoring the president of a local bank. Next to the photo of the man and his wife and daughter was a photo of that same daughter—quite pretty, as MaryBelle had said—dancing with his brother.

James groaned. The only good thing about the picture was that the woman's head completely blocked his brother's face from the photographer. Underneath it, they'd written that Sandra Hall, daughter of the honoree, danced with her escort for the evening, local actor Bobby Dillon.

Maybe Elise wouldn't see it.

The chances of that, when she'd already said she read the paper every day, weren't good. But if she didn't read the fine print under the picture, she'd never think that was him. He and Bobby looked alike—but when all the camera caught was broad shoulders and dark hair, it could be any one of a hundred men.

"Isn't she pretty?"

"What?" He looked up, startled by MaryBelle's question. "Oh, oh, yes, she's pretty."

"Have you met her?"

He couldn't remember if he'd been introduced to the young woman when he'd been at the school. It didn't matter. The only thing that mattered was whether Elise saw the paper.

"Uh, yeah, maybe."

The phone rang.

He leaped to his feet and grabbed the receiver. "Hello?" he said.

"At least you're awake this morning. That's more than I was when the phone rang," Bobby complained.

"What are you talking about?"

"The strange phone call I just got." Bobby stopped to yawn.

"Bobby, tell me about the call."

"A woman called. Asked for you. I told her you weren't here. She wanted to know where to find you. Sounded angry, bro. Did you do some lady wrong?"

"Did you give her this number?"

"Yeah. Sorry if you didn't want that."

About that time, he heard the beep signifying another call. "Uh, no, that's fine. I think this is her now. You didn't say anything else?"

"Hell, no. I was barely awake."

"Okay, thanks, Bobby." Then he clicked the button to take the next call. "Hello?"

"James?" a cold voice asked.

"Morning, Elise. How are you?"

Silence. Then she said, "We need to talk."

"I'll be right over. It'll take a few minutes—"

"No. Meet me at the coffee shop in half an hour."

And she hung up.

Chapter Seven

She'd made a mistake.

In fact, Elise figured she'd made so many mistakes in the past few days, she didn't have enough fingers to count them.

The worst one was underestimating James's ability to act. All those kisses yesterday had her drifting into a fantasyland where he wanted her, cared about her, tempted her.

And it had all been a sham. The photo had proven that. He'd left yesterday afternoon because he'd had a hot date that night. Had she already told her sisters about her "fiancé," her ruse would've been revealed.

How humiliating it would've been if one of her sisters had called the picture to her attention instead of Phoebe. She and Daisy had converged on Elise's apartment this morning.

Usually they walked to a nearby church for services, so Elise had suspected nothing when the two of them had arrived. But the frown on Phoebe's face, the sympathy in Daisy's eyes, had alerted her.

She took a booth in the coffee shop, ordering a diet cola and a roll while she waited for James. She'd planned her speech carefully. After all, the idea had been a crazy one, so the fault was hers. She felt no anger toward James, she assured herself as she crumpled her napkin into a tight ball. No anger at all.

James came through the door, a frown on his handsome forehead, and spotted her at once. He waved the hostess aside and hurried over to join her.

"Coffee, sir?" the waitress asked as soon as he'd sat down.

"Uh, yeah, thanks." He looked at the roll on Elise's plate. "And bring me one of those."

"Elise—" he began.

"Good morning, James," she said stiffly. *Remember, no anger at all.* "Thank you for finding the time to meet with me. I think we'd better rethink our plan. If—"

"No, that's not necessary," he protested.

She drew a deep breath. "Perhaps from your point of view it's not necessary, but I find it not only necessary but urgent."

"Let me explain."

"That's not necessary. As I was saying, if you haven't incurred expenses that exceed the five hundred dollars I've already paid, I think we should dissolve our agreement."

He opened his mouth to argue, she supposed, but the waitress arrived with his cup of coffee and roll.

Trying to remain calm, to show none of the hurt she didn't want to admit, she said, "I appreciate the effort you've put into our little scheme, but perhaps you can look upon it as a learning experience."

He reached across the table to grasp her hand. She tugged on it, determined to be free of him, and her elbow knocked over her cola. Rivulets of the drink rushed to the edge of the table and fell right into Elise's lap, like a dark waterfall.

"Oh, no!" she exclaimed, sliding out of the booth, trying to dab at the liquid with her tightly wadded napkin.

"Here, let me help," James urged, using his napkin to wipe her skirt.

The waitress hurried over, along with a second employee, both wanting to help, too. In no time, everyone in the restaurant was staring at them.

Elise closed her eyes. She wanted to be somewhere else, anywhere else. She wanted to turn back the clock to the day she got the brilliant idea to hire James Dillon. She wanted to be heart-whole, again.

"No!" she exclaimed, stopping all the activity around her.

"But, ma'am, if we get the excess liquid mopped up, maybe it won't stain," the waitress explained.

"No, I know. It's fine. The dress is washable. I'll go home at once and wash it. It doesn't matter. That's what I meant. It doesn't matter."

"I'll come with you," James assured her. "I'll help."

The two waitresses raised their eyebrows, obviously imagining James helping her disrobe, Elise decided. Great. Now her reputation would be ruined. Or enhanced. It depended on how a person looked at it.

"No, thank you. I'll manage."

"But we haven't finished talking," he protested.

"Oh, yes, we have. If you have any more expenses, you can mail them to me." She tried to keep her voice brisk, businesslike, instead of sounding as if she was about to burst into tears.

"Damn it, this isn't about expenses!" James shouted.

"Yes, it is!" she returned in a hoarse whisper, hoping not to draw too much attention to herself, though that was a ridiculous concern at this point.

"Elise!" a young woman just coming in screamed.

She couldn't believe her luck. Her next youngest sister, Melanie, had entered the coffee shop.

Her sister ran to her side, giving her a quick hug. "Oops! You have an accident, big sister?"

"I spilled my cola. Don't make a big deal, Mel. I'm on my way home to wash it. So if you'll excuse me—"

"Hi, I'm glad to finally meet some of Elise's family," James said, his deep, silky voice filling her with foreboding. She knew what was coming next, but she couldn't think fast enough to avoid it.

"Hi," Melanie said with a smile, her gaze roaming James's impressive physique and handsome face in appreciation. "Who are you?"

"I'm your sister's fiancé, James Dillon."

Elise wanted to slug him.

ELISE'S SISTER SCREAMED. "No! Oh, how wonderful! Elise, you rat! You never said a word. And here we were all worrying about you. How long? I mean, when is the wedding?"

"There's no—" Elise began, clearly hoping to straighten things out before they got worse.

"She says there's no hurry. I think she didn't want

to draw attention from your youngest sister's wedding, so we're waiting until after that event,'' James explained, wrapping his arm around Elise's shoulders and smiling at Melanie.

''Heck, Mom will be so ecstatic, she won't care when the wedding is. She's been so worried about Elise. She never—well, at least, that's what we thought. Elise, you sly creature!''

James ignored Elise's glare. She wasn't being terribly cooperative, but he'd worked with uncooperative people before. ''Look, she's pretty uncomfortable being the center of attention—and having a big wet spot on her dress, so we'd better go, but it was great meeting you. I'll see the rest of you at the wedding.''

He reached in his pocket and tossed a twenty down on the tabletop. The waitress, still standing there, said, ''I'll get your change, sir.''

''No need. Thanks for your assistance.'' Then he rushed Elise from the shop.

Elise went along with him, much to his relief, until they were outside the coffee shop. Then she dug in her heels like a stubborn mule.

''Come on, Elise, let me take you home so you can change,'' he urged.

''This is my car. I'll take myself home, thank you very much, you—you Benedict Arnold!''

''Benedict Arnold?'' he asked, his eyebrows slipping up. ''I haven't betrayed you. I did exactly what you hired me to do.''

''We'd agreed to call it off!''

''No, *I* hadn't agreed. And you had refused to listen to me. That was unfair!''

He almost grinned at the frustration on her face when she ground her teeth and glared at him. He asked, "Are you sure you're calm enough to drive?"

"I'll be a lot calmer when you let go of me and go away," she assured him.

"Okay, I'll get my car and follow you home."

"Don't bother! I never want to see you again."

She twisted out of his hold, ran to her car, and, before he knew it, had driven away.

He thought about following her, but he decided it would be better to wait an hour or two until she'd calmed down. Besides, he needed to talk to Bobby.

His brother was sitting at the kitchen table talking to MaryBelle, finishing off his uneaten breakfast, when James arrived home. He snagged the last muffin off the plate just before Bobby's hand reached it.

"Hey, I was going to eat that!" Bobby complained.

"Tough. As much trouble as you've caused me this morning, I should at least get a little breakfast."

MaryBelle looked surprised. "But I thought you were having breakfast at the coffee shop near the campus."

"I thought I was, too, but I didn't even get a sip of coffee."

"Their service has always been slow," MaryBelle said, nodding her head in sympathy.

"It wasn't the service. We had a—a little disagreement."

"With your new girlfriend?" his housekeeper asked in consternation. "Does that mean you're going to start growling again?"

"New girlfriend?" Bobby asked at the same time.

James sat down in a chair. "MaryBelle, could you bring me a cup of coffee? I need caffeine."

"You're dating again?" Bobby asked, as MaryBelle moved to respond to his request.

"Sort of," James answered cautiously. If Elise didn't forgive him for Bobby's newspaper appearance, he wasn't sure she'd ever speak to him again.

MaryBelle put a cup of coffee in front of him, and he gratefully took a sip. "Umm, good coffee. Thanks, MaryBelle."

"Your brother's been seeing her for almost a week," she told Bobby.

"Five days," James corrected.

Bobby raised his eyebrows. "You're counting the days? Sounds serious."

"No!" James immediately answered, frowning. It wasn't serious…just fun. And he hadn't had fun in a long time. "Look, Bobby, I need you to promise me something."

"What's that? Not to flirt with your woman?" his brother teased with a grin.

"No, I want you to promise that you won't get your picture in the paper for the next two weeks, especially with your arms around another woman."

"Another woman? You mean someone other than Sandy? That won't happen. She's the only lady for me." Before James could answer, he added, "I'm thinking about asking her to marry me."

"No! No, don't do that!" James roared.

"Hey, she's wonderful. What do you have against her?" Bobby half rose to his feet, anger on his face.

James held up a hand. "Nothing! I'm sure she's

lovely, Bobby, but if you propose, the next thing you know your picture will be back in the paper.''

"What's this hang-up you've got with me getting a little publicity? That's what actors do,'' Bobby said, frowning.

James sighed and took another drink of coffee. "It's a long story.''

MaryBelle and Bobby looked at each other and then at James. "We've got time,'' they said together, and waited.

THE PHONE RANG AGAIN.

Elise groaned and hid her head under the sofa cushion. The first two calls had come while she was in the shower after stripping off the stained dress. Her mother and one of her aunts had already heard the news. They couldn't wait to meet James. Melanie had told them how handsome he was.

When she'd played those messages, she hadn't known what to do. Before she could decide, the phone rang again. Afraid to answer it until she'd worked out a plan, she listened to one of her sisters gush about the news.

This last one was Sharon, her baby sister, calling to let her know she'd added James to the guest list, of course, and she'd reserve a room for him at the Hilton in Flagstaff, where the wedding would take place.

When the doorbell rang just as her sister hung up on the answering machine, Elise was sure it had to be more relatives—maybe her father, demanding details. But she had to answer the door, because the person kept pounding on it.

"I'm coming," she called out, hoping her visitor hadn't drawn her neighbors' interest. She swung open the door and then tried to close it again.

James Dillon, the source of all her difficulties, wouldn't let her. "Come on, Elise, let me in so we can talk. You need to hear what I have to say."

"Why bother? You spoke too much at the coffee shop."

"Please?" he asked, still holding the door open.

She heard another door open down the hall and she didn't want an audience for their conversation. "Fine. Come in."

James entered the apartment and closed the door behind him. "Will you listen to me?"

"Do I have a choice?"

"No. Sandy is an old family friend. I promised several months ago to escort her to the party because—because she and her boyfriend broke up, and she didn't have anyone to take her. She said it would be humiliating to go without an escort."

She stared at him, saying nothing.

"It's the same thing I'm doing for you, only I did it because I'm her friend, not for money."

"Bully for you," Elise grumbled.

"Look, I didn't even know they were taking pictures. Her mother told them who I was. The picture was as much a surprise to me as it was to you."

"That doesn't change the fact that it could've ruined everything if I'd already told my sisters about you," she pointed out.

"Why? You call me James. They wouldn't have connected the two since no one could see my face."

It irritated her, but he had a point.

"If they ask questions, I'll tell them Bobby is my younger brother."

Elise reminded herself what a good actor he was. He sounded so sincere that even she believed him, and she knew he was really Bobby. Oh, yeah, he'd definitely be a success in Hollywood. He was as fake as the town itself.

"When are you moving to Hollywood?" she abruptly asked.

"What are you talking about?"

"Aren't you moving to Hollywood, to find better roles? That's what every actor has in mind, isn't it?" She squared her jaw in stubbornness.

"What does that have to do with our situation?"

"Nothing. I just wondered." She wondered how she'd remember that he was playacting. She wondered how she would protect her heart. She wondered if she was going crazy.

"Please, Elise, let's continue the charade until after your sister's wedding, just like we planned."

"No, I—"

The phone interrupted her.

She sat on the couch, waiting.

"Aren't you going to answer it?"

She glared at him just as her mother's voice came from the answering machine. "Darling, I just happened to think. Why don't you bring James to dinner on Wednesday night? Your father wants to meet him, and we'll be so busy at the wedding we won't have a chance to get to know him. Call me back as soon as you can. I'll need to know his favorite foods. Bye."

"Your mother knows?" James asked.

"My family can spread gossip faster than a speeding bullet. Superman has nothing on them," Elise said, her voice filled with frustration. "That's Mother's second call. All six sisters and one aunt have already—"

The phone rang again.

"This has to be Aunt Lilly. I haven't heard from her yet," she said with a sigh.

"Darling Elise, this is Aunt Lilly," the answering machine said as if on cue. "I just heard the news— and I hear he's absolutely delicious. Leave it to you to only choose the best. I can't wait to meet him. Give him a kiss for me. Bye."

"I think I like Aunt Lilly," James said, and slid closer to her on the sofa.

Elise stiff-armed him. "Don't get carried away. There's no one here to convince." She closed her eyes. "I need time to think!"

When she felt movement, she snapped her eyes open, afraid James was ignoring her warning. Instead, he'd stood as if he was leaving.

"What's to think about, Elise? Your plan is working. And I promise to keep away from all other women until after the wedding, so there won't be any more pictures in the paper."

She closed her eyes again. His words, "until after the wedding," hurt almost as much as the picture had. She'd studied him with the blonde in his embrace. It was clear that the woman meant something to him. She'd be an idiot to fall for the line that she was just a friend. The look of contentment on the woman's face alone told of a deeper relationship, whether he knew it or not.

And she believed he did.

Body language was a lot more truthful than words.

But unless she wanted to upset the entire family, she'd take his offer of two weeks of monogamy. Then, when that time period was up, she'd have to walk away—without her heart broken, she hoped.

With an exhausted sigh, she said, "Okay, fine, we'll keep the agreement, though I don't know why it matters to you." She glared at him.

He shrugged. "A job's a job."

Of course, the money. At least about that he was honest.

"Of course. Fine. I'll call you when I have the details about the wedding. Give me your address. My sister Sharon will need it. She's going to send you a wedding invitation." She picked up a pen and note-pad, and waited.

He opened his mouth and then closed it again.

"What's the matter? Afraid I'll stalk you when this is over? Afraid I don't know the difference between playacting and the real thing? I can assure you, Mr. Dillon, that I—

He pulled her up into his arms and covered her lips with his. When she tried to protest, he deepened the kiss, and Elise melted into his embrace, her arms going around his neck. He lifted his mouth and stared at her. Then, before she could protest—as she assured herself later she had intended to do—he kissed her again.

The man had major talent in the kissing department. She'd thought his acting was good, but his kissing was even better. So good, in fact, she forgot all about their pretense, his lies, the truth about their engagement. All she could think about was him.

When he finally ended the kiss, she stared at him as he picked up the pad and pen and quickly wrote something down. Then he leaned over and kissed her briefly.

"I'll call you tonight," he whispered, then walked out the door.

Oh mercy, she was in big trouble.

"DARLING, YOU NEVER called me back," her mother complained later over the phone.

"Oh, hello, Mother. I'm sorry. James was here and I waited until he left, but then I got busy with some chores and forgot."

"Well, that's not very flattering, dear. Can James come to dinner Wednesday night? We're dying to meet him."

"Oh, Mother, let's not. Things are going to be so hectic between now and the wedding. You'll meet him then. After the wedding, we'll have time to visit."

After the wedding, she'd tell her mother he'd gotten a role in Hollywood and had to leave. Her mother wouldn't want to stand in the way of his career advancement.

"We'll keep it simple, dear. Just the four of us. You certainly can't get engaged without introducing him to your father and me. He'll need to ask your father's permission, of course. Now, tell me what his favorite foods are. I want him to feel welcome."

"Mother, I—"

"I insist."

"Okay, fine. His favorite foods are—" She thought frantically. Then, with a smile, she said, "His favorite foods are cabbage and boiled potatoes."

"But, dear, none of us like that," her mother protested.

"I know," Elise agreed. With any luck, she figured James wouldn't, either.

Chapter Eight

The three friends sat at their usual table at The Prickly Pear.

"So, what happened with James?" Daisy asked.

Elise hadn't spoken with her friends since yesterday morning when they'd shown her the picture of James in the paper. "We're still pretending."

Phoebe leaned forward. "One of the chapters in that book says you should avoid lies."

Though still unnerved by the events of yesterday, Elise raised her eyebrows and looked Phoebe directly in the eye. "Then it's a good thing I'm not looking for a husband, isn't it?"

Phoebe grinned. "I guess so."

"Are you okay?" Daisy asked.

"Sure," Elise said. "In fact, I'm better than okay. I even managed to find another candidate for the Daddy job."

Daisy looked wary, but Phoebe was pleased.

"All right! Way to go, Elise."

"Not James, right?" Daisy asked. "It's someone else?"

"Of course, not James! He—he's too popular."

She thought of Sandy, the woman in the picture. Definitely too popular.

"Hey, I thought you and James were going to the movies tonight. Isn't that what you told me?" Phoebe suddenly asked.

"I canceled." She didn't add any details. Even to her friends she couldn't confess how close she'd come to losing all objectivity about James. There would be no more "research" evenings.

Except, of course, for Wednesday night when she had to take him to dinner at her parents'.

"Okay, so tell us about the new candidate," Phoebe ordered after a slight pause. "Is he handsome?"

"Not like James," she said without thinking. Then she hurriedly added, "I mean, he's not dark, he's a blonde."

"Blonde? Surfer type?" Daisy asked.

"No, not at all. He's a professor in the History Department. I thought about how I found James and I decided to check out the other departments. Not only is Dave one of the most popular history professors, but he's writing a book," Elise said, looking at Daisy, hoping for a positive reaction.

"Really?" Daisy asked, her eyes lighting up. "So, he's not all muscle."

Phoebe gave Elise an encouraging smile before saying to Daisy, "And you can't complain he puts his hands in people's mouths."

"True. And college professors don't have as demanding schedules as businessmen. He'd have more time for family," Daisy speculated. "When do I meet him?"

"Tonight. He promised to drop by. I thought it might be easier to meet him that way instead of on a blind date."

"That's great," Daisy agreed. "I hate blind dates."

"Oh, look, there's Frannie—" Phoebe pointed before waving at the red-haired figure in a clashing red sweater and black clam-diggers.

Frannie beamed at them and hurried over. "Hi! I was hoping I'd run into the three of you. I was feeling a little lonesome tonight, after our fun weekend."

"Join us, Frannie," Elise offered, pulling out the fourth chair.

"Have you ordered yet?" Frannie asked, sitting down and picking up a menu at the same time.

"Not yet. George went to get our drinks, but he'll be back in a minute." Elise, sitting facing the door, kept watching for Dave, the history professor.

That's why she immediately saw the two men who entered. She knew both of them. James Dillon and Bill White. By the way they stood at the door, their gazes sweeping the room, she knew they were looking for someone in particular. She didn't wave.

They found her, anyway, and headed across the room.

Frannie, looking up from the menu, noticed Bill at once. "Look who's here," she whispered fiercely. She half rose in her chair. "Yoo-hoo, Bill. Hello!"

Bill's cheeks turned bright red and he gave a half wave. James didn't even smile, his gaze fixed on Elise.

"James is with Bill," Daisy said. "Did you know he was coming?"

Elise shook her head.

"Evening, ladies," James said, having reached the table. "Mind if Bill and I join you?"

"Of course not," Phoebe said, standing. "We'll just need to pull over that empty table and put it with this one. Frannie, why don't you move down here with me, and they can add a table."

Elise almost smiled at Frannie's eager response. Her move would put her next to one of the men. Elise would be pleased if it was James, but probably Frannie would make sure it was Bill.

James helped move the other table over. Then he pulled up a chair next to Elise.

"What are you doing here?" she whispered fiercely. She'd told him last night there would be no more "research" evenings.

"I stopped by to talk to Bill, and he suggested we eat here," he said, smiling slightly, daring her to accuse him of lying.

She glared at him. "And why did you stop by to talk to Bill?"

"Not that it's any of your business, Elise, but I read a police report about thefts in the neighborhood, and I thought I should let Bill know, so he could be on the alert."

Frannie had been listening. "Thefts? Oh, no. I won't be able to sleep tonight."

Bill, having sat down beside Frannie, shook his head. "I don't think we're in any danger. The lighting helps deter crime."

"I'm sure you're right," Phoebe agreed.

"And it helps that all the men in our units are big

and strong,'' Frannie said with fluttering lashes and a sideways look at Bill.

"Elise?"

Elise whirled around, embarrassed to discover Dave Haskell standing beside her. She'd gotten so distracted by James's arrival, she'd forgotten to watch for Daisy's potential date.

"Oh, Dave, I'm glad you found us. Please join us," she said at once, smiling as she stood and welcomed him.

James stood beside her, frowning. "Hello, I'm James Dillon, Elise's fiancé." He stuck out his hand.

Dave looked at Elise in surprise, but shook James's hand. "Dave Haskell."

Elise quickly introduced the rest of the table, saving Daisy until last. Dave's smile widened slightly as he shook her hand. Then he scooted his chair right next to her.

Elise and Phoebe exchanged a look of triumph.

"Is he the one?" James whispered in her ear.

She drew away from him even as she shivered. "What do you mean?"

"Did you invite him for Daisy? To father her child?"

The man had the memory of an elephant. With a slight nod, she turned to Dave. "How did your classes go today?"

"Fine. My freshman class actually stayed awake today," the man said, smiling at Daisy. "It was one of my good days."

Bill looked at Dave. "You teach at the university with Elise?"

"Well, not in the same department. I teach History and she teaches French."

Bill nodded. "Then you must know James, too. He's in the Drama Department."

FOR THE FIRST TIME that night, James thought his brilliant idea to talk Bill into coming with him to The Prickly Pear wasn't so brilliant.

Dave was staring at him.

"ASU is big, Bill. We don't all know each other," James hurriedly said.

"He's right," Dave said. "I've heard of a Bobby Dillon in the Drama Department, but I haven't actually met him. Any kin?"

Before James could answer, Elise said, "That's James's stage name."

Dave nodded.

George arrived with the three women's drinks. "Looks like the party has grown. Can I get drinks for anyone else?"

As they went around the table, James leaned closer to Elise. "I assume that's diet cola?"

She nodded. "Yes, and don't get near it. I don't want another cola bath."

"A little too much excitement for you?" he asked.

She glared at him.

"And you, sir?" George asked, looking at James.

"I'll have a cup of coffee."

"Fine. I'll be right back with your drinks and then I'll take your orders."

James wasn't in any rush. Now that disaster had been avoided with the newcomer, he wanted to prolong the evening. He was pretty sure Elise wouldn't ask him to go back to her apartment with her.

"About Wednesday night—" he began, leaning closer to her again just so he could smell her perfume.

"Say, James," Dave said at the same time, "how long have you been at the university?"

James was forced to deal with Dave's question, but he hadn't come tonight to discuss his brother's life. He wanted to talk to Elise.

"Uh, I came back last year."

"Came back?"

James sighed. "I worked for a couple of years before I came back to get my Masters. Have you visited Daisy's shop?" Okay, so his change of subject wasn't smooth, but he didn't want to answer the man's questions. And he didn't like the way the guy kept looking at Elise.

He was supposed to be concentrating on Daisy.

He caught a look from Phoebe that said she could read him like a book. He sure hoped not.

The rest of the evening, Dave did concentrate on Daisy. But it didn't encourage Elise to concentrate on James. In fact, she did her best to ignore him. But he hung in there. He intended to convince her they needed more time together to make their story believable.

"Did you and Phoebe and Daisy drive over together?" he asked as they were getting ready to leave.

"Yes."

"Let me drive you home. I have a couple of questions I need to ask you." All he'd have to do if she agreed was come up with some questions. He could do that.

"I'll be able to answer them on the way to my parents' house on Wednesday. You haven't forgotten, have you?"

"Of course not. I'm looking forward to it. But that's why I need my questions answered."

"Elise, are you ready?" Phoebe asked.

"I'm taking her home," James immediately said.

"Yes, I'm ready," Elise said to Phoebe. "I'm going with you and Daisy."

Daisy was talking quietly to Dave, so Phoebe came around the table to where James and Elise stood. "Should we stall?" she whispered.

"We could stage an argument to give them more time," James suggested. "Elise is really good with arguments."

She glared at him.

Phoebe chuckled. "Maybe she's been inspired."

"Oh, I have," Elise said fervently. "And while we're waiting, I remember something I need to tell you."

"Oh?" he asked warily, not trusting the glint in her eyes.

"Yes. Daddy is expecting to speak with you privately."

He frowned. "Why?"

"Why, for you to ask for my hand in marriage, of course. Unless you've changed your mind." Then she sailed out the door, followed by a chuckling Phoebe.

James was still standing there, in shock, when Daisy told him goodbye.

"Are you okay?" she asked.

"Yeah. Oh, and give Elise a message for me."

"Yes?"

"Tell her I'll be ready. I haven't changed my mind," he said with a grim smile. "She'll know what I mean."

HE COULDN'T BELIEVE he was nervous.

Even when he'd proposed to Sylvia, he hadn't sweated.

Now, he felt as if he must have lost five pounds on the drive to pick up Elise. For so long, he'd depended on his money and his power to pave the way for him. But neither Elise nor her parents knew anything about those things in connection to him.

In their minds, he was just a guy—a guy with a very low-paying job, asking to marry their daughter.

He wondered how Bobby would ever find the courage to ask Sandy's parents. James was having difficulty with it, even though it was only a pretense.

Elise had suggested she meet him at her parents', but he'd vetoed that idea. He wasn't about to arrive alone. When he knocked on her apartment door, she opened it, and he took a deep breath.

She was wearing green again.

Without thinking, he reached for her, eager to greet her with a kiss.

She backed away.

"Ready?" he asked, his voice husky. At least when they got to her parents', she couldn't refuse to let him touch her.

"Yes." She reached for a small handbag on the

lamp table. Then she led the way out of her apartment.

She kept a determined silence, only answering in monosyllables any question he asked.

Finally, he gave up talking about their relationship and switched to Daisy's. A topic she couldn't resist. "How are things going with Dave and Daisy?"

"I don't know. She doesn't seem enthusiastic, but she hasn't said there's anything wrong with him."

"What do you mean?"

"Well, for the dentist, she had a list of his faults. She hasn't done that with Dave. All she's said is there's no spark."

Like there was between them. A spark he'd never felt before. A flame that burned inside him, unnoticed until he got near Elise, when it became a bonfire.

"Don't you think that's a problem?"

"Of course, it's a problem!" Elise snapped. "But I don't know what to do about it. How can you predict when—when that spark will appear? It's not rational!"

"I know what you mean," he agreed. Sometimes it was damn inconvenient.

"So, are you still looking for someone else?" he finally asked.

"Of course. We want Daisy to be happy."

"What does that book say?"

"Keep your eyes open."

The advice sounded cryptic to James. "What does that mean?"

"Daisy's having a showing this evening at her shop. An artist who's become very popular is going to be there with some of his new paintings. Phoebe's going. She figures there might be some men there alone.''

"So she'll walk up to them and ask if they want to be a daddy?" he asked, smiling as he imagined that scenario.

"No, of course not!"

"Good, because looking at Phoebe, they might volunteer before she can point out Daisy."

"You think Phoebe's beautiful?"

Uh-oh. He heard something in Elise's voice that told him he'd made a mistake. She couldn't be jealous, could she? "No more than you or Daisy," he said, trying to keep his voice casual.

"Then why—"

"Sweetheart, if any of you come on to a man, he's not going to start looking around for another woman. He's going to thank his lucky stars and grab you." His imagination was going crazy. He cleared his throat. "So don't go asking any other men to be a daddy, okay?"

"I don't intend to. But you're wrong. A mention of future children tends to make a man back away. At least, that's what I've heard." She stared straight ahead.

She was right. Talk about children had always had that effect on him, come to think of it. Not because he didn't want children, but because he hadn't wanted commitment to any woman after Sylvia.

Until now.

No, he hurriedly assured himself, that wasn't true. Because Elise wasn't wanting commitment. That's why he was so relaxed. Not because he wanted to commit to her. No, it wasn't that.

"So, what's Phoebe going to say to them?"

"She's planning on being subtle, James," Elise said, her voice dry. "She'll start up a conversation about the art on display. We both think a man interested in art might be exactly what Daisy needs."

Somehow, James didn't have much faith in Phoebe's plan. But as long as it didn't involve Elise approaching strange men, he'd keep his opinion to himself.

"Turn right at the light," Elise ordered.

Suddenly, James remembered what he had before him. "Uh, when am I supposed to talk to your dad? Before dinner, or after?"

"I don't know. Does it matter?" She threw him a sharp glare, and he tried to look calm.

"Of course not."

"James, are you nervous?"

"Don't be ridiculous. This is just another acting gig. It doesn't mean anything." He didn't dare reveal the anxiety he was feeling. She might wonder why.

"Okay. You can do it before or after dinner. Whichever you prefer."

"Okay, I'll do it before I sit down to eat with them. I'll admit to being a little tense. Don't want to spoil my appetite," he said, trying a chuckle.

A secret smile played across Elise's beautiful lips. "Oh, I wouldn't worry about that."

"Elise, what are you up to?"

"What do you mean?" she asked, turning to look at him, her green eyes wide.

Then she directed him to turn in at the next driveway. Before she could get out of the car, however, he caught her arm.

"Wait just a minute. Tell me what you meant."

"James, we can't sit out here. They'll have been watching for us. They'll think we're—" She broke off, her cheeks red.

"Making out? They'll think I can't keep my hands off you? Yeah, that's what they'll think. So tell me what you meant before they think we're indulging in a quickie."

"James Dillon! How dare you—"

He planted a kiss on her open mouth and put into the kiss all the hunger he'd felt since Saturday.

When he finally lifted his head, he said, "You want to tell me now?"

"No," she said, shoving away from him. She slipped out of the car before he could stop her.

But he'd definitely accomplished one thing. She looked decidedly kissed—like he couldn't keep his hands off her.

Once inside, she introduced her parents. He liked them both. Her mother resembled Elise, except that she was much calmer. Mr. Foster was a genial man, welcoming him with a smile.

"Call me Sam," he said as James greeted him.

"Thank you, Sam. I appreciate you and your wife inviting me over. I'm glad to finally meet you."

"Likewise, son, likewise. Too bad we couldn't have the whole family over. They're all dying to meet you. But Margaret said you'd be overwhelmed." He eyed James, and James straightened, trying to look comfortable but in control.

"Not sure Margaret was right. You look like you can handle yourself.

"I've had some experience in several areas."

Elise and her mother were walking toward what he guessed was the kitchen. James leaned forward to say quietly, ''I wonder if this might not be a good time for us to have a private chat.''

The look of surprise on the man's face, and a smile on Elise's face as she looked over her shoulder, made James wonder if she'd just played a trick on him.

Chapter Nine

Sam Foster led the way down a hallway and opened a door.

"In here. This is my room. No ladies allowed." He grinned. "Which means it may not be too clean."

"No problem," James assured his host. His mouth suddenly seemed to be stuffed with cotton. He hated the thought of lying to this man.

After they both sat down, Sam smiled encouragingly but said nothing.

James cleared his throat, then opened his mouth.

Nothing came out.

"Don't be nervous, James," Sam said. "It is James, isn't it?"

James stiffened. "Of course."

Sam grinned. "I thought so. The two of you look a lot alike, but you're older, more the age for Elise."

"The two of us?" James asked, his voice hoarse from strain.

"You and Bobby. Elise said something about Bobby being your stage name, but why would an advertising executive need a stage name?"

James swallowed a large lump in his throat. "Uh, you—you know about my agency?"

"Of course. Looked you up on the Internet." Sam beamed at him and waved his hand toward the computer sitting on his desk. "My son, Chance, bought that for me my last birthday. He's been teaching me how to use it. I can e-mail!"

James nodded approval as his mind frantically tried to figure out how to deal with this latest revelation.

"I put in both names and got pictures of two different guys, you and Bobby, but I figured you were kin because you looked alike. I guess Margaret got things wrong."

"Uh, did you—did you tell anyone? Margaret or anyone?" James held his breath while the man considered his answer.

"Nope, can't say I have. My wife loves to hear herself talk. She's been discussing you nonstop. She wouldn't believe me, anyhow."

James leaned forward. "Sam, we need to talk."

"That's what we're doing, isn't it?"

"Yeah, but now we've *really* got to talk."

"WHERE DID the men go?" Margaret asked as she carried a bowl of boiled potatoes to the table.

"I think Dad took James back to his room."

"Oh, mercy, the poor man is going to think I'm a terrible housekeeper. Your father won't let me touch that room. Says he's afraid I'll mess up his computer. Like he'd know the difference!"

"It's all right, Mom. James won't mind a little dust. I see you fixed the boiled potatoes." Elise couldn't help smiling, hoping James hated the dishes as much as she did.

"Yes, and the cabbage, too. But I didn't fix much. You know your father hates it. So I made meat loaf and green bean casserole. And I made a chocolate cake—my double-chocolate, three-layer cake. All your brothers-in-law love it."

"Yes, I know, Mom." Elise was feeling worse about her dirty trick now. Her mother prided herself on her cooking. She would be more disappointed than James when he didn't like her cuisine.

Elise looked over her shoulder, but there was no sign of James or her father. Did that mean they were getting along? Of course, her father could get along with almost anyone.

Growing more nervous by the minute, she turned to her mother. "Should I go call Dad and James? We wouldn't want the food to get cold."

Her mother surveyed the carefully set table. "Of course, dear. Oh! I almost forgot the salad I made." She whirled around and headed for the kitchen.

Now Elise really felt rotten. Her mother had used her best china, put her favorite tablecloth on the table, the one she had to iron. Margaret had gone to a lot of trouble, and the evening was going to be a disaster.

Elise needed to talk to James, to promise him whatever he wanted if he'd pretend to like boiled potatoes and cabbage.

She hurried down the hall and rapped on the closed door. "Dad? James? Mom says dinner's ready."

When her father opened the door, Elise hurriedly

studied his face. He gave her a broad smile. "Good! We've worked up an appetite." Then, much to her surprise, he hugged her tightly. "Everything's going to be all right."

She was still standing there, staring after him as he headed to the dining room, when James spoke.

"Nice man."

She whipped her head back around. "Yes. Yes, he is. A good father."

"I could tell."

"Uh, James," Elise began, bringing her mind back to the difficulty. "I need a favor."

"Okay."

She straightened her shoulders. She hated confessing what she'd done. "I told Mom your favorite foods are boiled potatoes and cabbage."

Staring at her, he shuddered. "You think I'm Irish?" he asked, grinning.

"No. I was—angry with you."

He stepped closer and took her hands. "I guess I can understand that. What's the favor?"

She licked her lips. "I want you to pretend to like cabbage and potatoes."

He stared at her, saying nothing.

"Please, James? I didn't think. Mom went to a lot of trouble to make the dinner what she thought you wanted. She's going to be so disappointed."

"Cabbage?" was his only response.

"Come on, James. You're an actor. Please? I'll owe you."

"Hmm. What are you offering in return?"

"I don't know." She tried to think of something

she could do for him, but she was pretty sure he didn't want to learn French verb conjugations.

A smile began on his face, then built to a radiance that matched the twinkle in his blue eyes. She began to worry.

"Okay. I'll pretend to love cabbage and potatoes. And for every bite I take, I get one kiss."

"Every bite? A kiss for every bite?" She drew a deep breath. "No! That's ridiculous!"

Though his smile dimmed, it remained on his face. "Okay. No problem."

"You'll do it, anyway?" she asked hopefully.

"Not a chance. I hate cabbage." He actually moved around her to head for the dining room.

"James! I'll pay you."

"I told you what I wanted."

He stood waiting for an answer.

Elise tried to think of something else to offer, but she couldn't come up with anything. Finally, drawing a deep breath, she asked, "Just kisses? Nothing else?"

"Sweetheart, your kisses will be about all I can handle, they're so potent." His smile brightened as he watched her.

"Okay." She raised her chin. "But *I'm* the one keeping count!"

JAMES FIGURED he earned every kiss he intended to collect that night. But after ten bites, by his count, he decided he couldn't handle any more. Particularly since he'd used bites of meat loaf to disguise the cabbage.

The potatoes were good, but filling. With the addition of the tasty green bean casserole, James fig-ured he'd eaten enough for a week. Then his hostess brought out a giant chocolate cake.

He tried to decline a piece, but Elise caught his eye, and he knew what she wanted. Not that he in-tended to charge her for the bites of cake. He'd throw those in for free.

When it came time to leave and Margaret kissed his cheek and welcomed him to the family, he felt bad. He and Sam exchanged handshakes. Sam had been remarkably understanding.

When he and Elise got in MaryBelle's car, she muttered something.

He drove out of the driveway before he asked for a repeat.

"I said, thank you."

"You're welcome. Ten."

"Ten? What do you mean?"

He stopped at a red light and turned to look at her. "You know what I mean. I took ten bites."

"You only took five. I watched."

"Five of cabbage. And five of potatoes. That makes ten."

"But you don't hate potatoes!"

He grinned. "Nope, but I don't usually eat a lot of them. Besides, you didn't specify only cabbage. You asked me to pretend to like both of them." He watched her struggle. It amazed him. Sylvia wouldn't have hesitated to lie. She had not liked to lose…anything.

"Are you sure you're not a lawyer? Specializing in contracts?"

"I'm sure. By the way, your parents are great people."

"Yes, thank you. I regret deciding to do this…deception. I don't like lying to them."

"I know what you mean. But you do have a good reason," he pointed out. Her father had agreed. He'd told James he worried about Elise.

"I guess. I think I was too much of a wimp to stand up to them. But it's gone so far now, I don't think I can call it off. Until after the wedding."

He could feel her staring at him. He didn't look at her as he made a turn.

"You do realize you're going to disappear after the wedding, don't you?"

"Sure. I'm going to Hollywood, right?" He tried to sound unconcerned, but somehow he was reluctant to consider the future. He was enjoying himself with Elise's little masquerade. That was all, of course. He didn't want anything serious.

But he did want to collect his kisses.

Anticipation rose as he pulled into a parking space by Mesa Blue. She reached for her door handle.

"Whoa, young lady. You've got a debt to pay."

"Tonight?" she asked, a panicky look on her face.

"Tonight. I don't believe in long-term debt." Not when he'd been anticipating those kisses for several hours. She still held on to the door handle. "Of course, we can settle the debt in your apartment, if you want. There's more room, more…privacy there."

"No! No, I'll pay up here."

He was actually glad she didn't invite him upstairs. With a bed in the vicinity, he wasn't sure he'd be able to keep his promise to limit their encounter only to kisses. When he touched her, every thought went out of his head.

"Okay. But you have to part company with the door, sweetheart. I don't think my lips can find yours if you don't."

He gave thanks for MaryBelle's car as he slid from under the steering wheel on the bench seat. His Mercedes had bucket seats. The leather might be softer than the plastic-covered seat of MaryBelle's car, but necking wouldn't be nearly as much fun.

"You promised only kisses," she reminded him as he reached for her.

He frowned. "You mean, I can't hold you?"

She solemnly shook her head, staring at him.

"Okay, just lips. But come closer."

She moved an inch away from the door.

"Come on, Elise, play fair." He watched as she scooted closer. Again he thought of Sylvia. No way would she play fair. She never had.

When Elise finally moved to within a couple of inches, he slowly, gently, touched his lips to hers. Soft lips, tender, relenting, settled against his with a sigh. Slowly he increased the pressure, teasing her lips into opening to him.

When he finally lifted his head, he muttered, "That's one."

He noted her green eyes were dazed when she asked, "One what?"

"Never mind," he whispered, and set his lips on hers again.

By the fourth kiss, her arms were around his neck and he was caressing every part of her he could reach. And wishing for her bed. Her touch was magic—potent magic that made him forget any warnings he might have made to himself, any promises he'd given her.

When she finally broke away from him, he'd lost count of the kisses, but he was sure he had a few more coming. At least, he prayed he did. It would be like cutting off a man's food source, leaving him to starve, if he didn't.

"Elise," he whispered as she shoved against him.

"No! No, that's enough," she said, her breathing rapid and shallow. "We have to stop!"

He guessed she was right. But right now, he thought stopping was the dumbest idea anyone had ever had.

"Elise—"

She wasn't listening. Instead, she'd grabbed the door handle, opened the door and was getting out.

He hurriedly did the same, coming around the car to stop her escape. "Wait. I'll—I'll call you tomorrow."

"No! Don't call. I don't want to talk to you."

With a frown, he asked, "Then when will we get together next? You know, to—to make sure—"

"No more research. Do your research with Sandra," she snapped. "I'll call you when I have the details about the wedding. That's all."

She turned and ran, leaving him standing by his car, shocked and disappointed.

BY FRIDAY, Elise had recovered from her necking session with James. If she didn't think about it.

It was two days later, and her breathing would

grow labored, her heart would race and a yearning would fill her stomach if she let her mind drift to the time spent in James's arms.

"Ridiculous!" she muttered under her breath.

"Did you say something?" Phoebe asked.

"Um, no. When will Daisy get here?"

"She called and said she'd meet us here at your place at six-thirty. She had to lock up and everything. Why? Are you hungry?"

They were all going to dinner together again.

"No. No, I'm just—impatient."

"I thought you'd be going out with James. I was surprised when Daisy said you were available." Phoebe cocked her head as she studied Elise. "Anything wrong?"

"Nothing's wrong. It—it was a long week." A difficult week. Time spent with James. Time spent without James. She couldn't figure out which was worse.

"Relax. I'm sure she'll be here soon. Has she been out with Dave? I thought they kind of connected Monday night."

"They're going out tomorrow night. But you heard her say there was no spark."

Phoebe shrugged. "Face it, Elise. Daisy is a romantic. You and I know there's no such thing as a 'spark.'"

Elise started to agree, but honesty wouldn't let her. Spark? There was more than that. With James, she felt as if she was being consumed by a fire. It didn't mean anything, of course. Except that they were attracted to each other.

"Um, well—"

"Elise!" a female voice screamed, and they could hear someone running down the hallway.

Both women sprang to the door. Elise stepped into the hallway to discover Frannie racing toward them. But instead of the panic and fear she'd expected to see on Frannie's face, Elise saw delight, joy.

"Frannie, what is it?"

"Heavens to Betsy," Phoebe added, "you scared us to death. I thought someone was after you."

"Maybe," Frannie said, beaming.

"Come in, Frannie, and make sense. Tell us what's going on," Elise ordered. Anything to keep her mind off James.

Frannie rushed past Elise and Phoebe into the apartment. Frannie always dressed so as to be noticed, but tonight she'd outdone herself. She was wearing a jersey top in lemon yellow, its wraparound style exposing a large part of her impressive bosom. She'd paired the shirt with red shorts. The shorts were actually modest in length, reaching her mid-thigh, but the legs were flared, the length shifting with every step.

She wore big gold hoops in her ears, and her hair was in another of those intricate beehives. Red-and-yellow high-heel sandals adorned her feet.

"Wow, you're dressed to kill tonight, Frannie," Phoebe commented, obviously seeing what Elise was seeing.

Frannie beamed at Phoebe. "Oh, yes. Thank you for noticing. Do you think Bill will, too?"

Elise blinked. "Bill? You're going out with Bill?" Frannie had longed for a date, a real date, with Bill

White, Mesa Blue's manager, for as long as Elise had known her.

But Bill was shy.

"I think he couldn't help but notice, Frannie," Elise said faintly.

Frannie flung her hands out and spun around, so Elise and Phoebe could see every inch of her. Then she clasped her hands over her chest in the region of her heart, and said, with great dramatic flair, "My fate is in your hands."

Elise looked behind her, sure Frannie must be talking to someone else. But no one was there. And Frannie was staring directly at her.

She was getting a bad feeling.

"What do you mean, Frannie?" Phoebe asked.

Frannie took a step closer to Elise. "You know how I've longed to have a date with Bill, don't you, Elise?"

"Yes, Frannie," Elise said slowly.

"Well, he's asked me out."

Daisy walked into the room, since they'd left the door open. "Hi. Who's asked you out?" she asked Frannie.

"Bill! My darling Bill!"

"Well, bully for you," Daisy cheered, but Elise noted that she seemed tired.

"But it all depends on Elise!" Frannie, back in dramatic mode, added.

All three of her companions turned to stare at Elise. "What are you talking about, Frannie? I don't know anything about Bill asking you out."

"I know. That's what I'm here to explain."

"And make it fast," Daisy said, falling to Elise's sofa with a sigh, "because I'm tired and hungry."

"It's quite simple." Frannie shook her head, jangling her big earrings. "Bill will take me out if Elise goes with us." She smiled at Elise, as if her words settled everything.

"That sounds suspicious," Phoebe said with a frown.

"Thank you for saying so," Elise said. "I thought maybe I'd gone crazy. Frannie, why would Bill want me to come along?"

"Because he's shy, of course."

Daisy raised the objection this time. "No man is that shy. Even Bill."

Frannie ignored Daisy. "Please say you'll come, Elise. It's my only chance."

"You know that's not true," Elise protested. "Bill—living in the same complex with Bill gives you lots of chances."

"They haven't done me any good so far. Please?"

"Okay, you and Bill can join us," Elise said. "We're going to The Prickly Pear for dinner, as usual. We'll enjoy having the two of you with us."

Elise sent an apologetic look at her friends. Not that they would object to helping Frannie. She knew them better than that. But they wouldn't be able to have a heart-to-heart the way they usually did. And she'd made the offer without consulting them.

Frannie squeezed her hands tightly together, tears filling her eyes. But instead of sounding grateful, she cried, "No! That won't do!"

Phoebe, Daisy and Elise stared at her.

"It won't?" Daisy asked.

"No. It can't be a group thing. It has to be a double date. A real date."

That foreboding Elise had had earlier came back.

Phoebe said, "I don't understand. If it's you, Bill and Elise, how is that like a real date?"

"Because you forgot James, of course!" Frannie exclaimed.

Chapter Ten

Elise began backing away from Frannie. "No. I'm not seeing James tonight."

Frannie came after her. "If you don't see James, I won't see Bill," she wailed.

Elise closed her eyes briefly. She'd promised herself she wouldn't have to deal with James and the raging attraction she couldn't seem to control until the wedding, when she'd be surrounded by family.

When she opened her eyes, she faced three pairs of pleading eyes.

"Come on, Elise," Phoebe said. "What's one more date with James? You've already been out with him several times. You said everything went well."

"Yeah, in the name of love," Daisy added with a grin. "You're trying to fix me up, but you don't even have to find the guy to fix Frannie up."

"You don't understand," Elise protested. "Even if I wanted to spend the evening with James, I can't call him on the spur of the moment and insist he cooperate. I don't even know if he's home." She thought her argument was valid and should satisfy everyone.

"You don't have to," Frannie assured her, excitement in her voice. "He and Bill are waiting in my apartment. They're all ready to go as soon as we get there."

Elise stared at Frannie. "How did that happen?" she asked, suspicion in her voice.

Phoebe stepped to her side. "It doesn't matter. However it happened, Frannie gets her chance with Bill."

Elise got the message. If she asked too many questions, Frannie might realize Bill hadn't initiated the date. Because there was no doubt in Elise's mind now. James had to have set this evening up.

She didn't know why. He was handsome enough. He could find a woman to make out with. Heck, he could make out with Sandra. From the picture she saw, Elise knew Sandra would have no objection.

But *she* did.

"I can't—I'm not dressed." She was in her beloved jeans with a knit top. Jeans that James loved.

"We're going casual," Frannie assured her, still smiling.

"I have to change," Elise muttered, and ran from the room. No way was she going to walk in front of James Dillon in her jeans.

Five minutes later she reappeared in a pair of baggy khakis and an extra-long blouse. Neither revealed much of what was underneath.

Frannie looked at her dubiously. "I think the jeans looked better."

Daisy tried to hide a chuckle. "I'd take her as she is, Frannie, unless you want her to cancel completely."

"Oh! Oh, you look—marvelous, Elise. Beige really becomes you."

Even Elise couldn't hold back a smile at Frannie's sudden reversal. "I get the message, Frannie. You'd tell the devil himself he looked cool if it got you a date with Bill."

Frannie blushed, a rare occurrence. "I really love him, Elise. I just haven't figured out a way to tell him. When he'll hardly speak to me, it seems a bit forward to move to the love stage in one leap."

"I know. Come on, let's go claim our dates." Elise put on a smile, all the while planning what she would say to James Dillon about his conniving behavior.

"I REALLY APPRECIATE your helping me out, Bill," James said to the older man as they waited for Frannie's return.

"I just hope it works, James. It's a shame you and Elise had a fight. I think you make a wonderful couple." Bill paused and cleared his throat. "I explained to Frannie so she wouldn't think I was, uh, hitting on her."

James was truly grateful Bill and Frannie were going along with his conspiracy. It not only allowed him to see the elusive Elise, it also provided great entertainment.

"Uh, maybe Frannie would like you to hit on her."

Bill looked away. "Aw, she's a flirt, but she's not interested in anything permanent."

"How do you know?"

"She dates a lot of guys. I don't know enough

about women to keep her happy. Better if I don't even try.''

"'Faint heart never won fair lady,'" James quoted.

"Oh, you actors know all the right words. Say, maybe you'd give me lessons about, you know, keeping a lady happy.''

James shook his head. "You're asking me for love lessons when I'm having to resort to trickery just to see Elise? I don't think I'd be much help."

"See," Bill said, shrugging his shoulders, "it's hopeless." He absently stroked one of Frannie's cats.

"Maybe we can help each other. Let's see how the evening goes." James had a sneaking suspicion Elise was going to be even angrier when she figured out what he'd done. He wasn't even sure she'd agree to the evening.

Footsteps on the stairs near Frannie's apartment caused him to tense. He'd soon know, one way or the other. He could hear Frannie's voice. It seemed she was talking to someone. He hoped it was Elise.

After the end of their evening Wednesday, he'd been able to think of little else. The need to at least talk to Elise had occupied his mind nonstop.

Who was he kidding? He didn't just want to talk to her. But by setting up the evening with chaperones, he could see her without being badly tempted.

"Bill, we're here. We're ready. Elise said she's starving," Frannie announced, a big smile on her face.

Elise, following her, wore a smile, too, but James wasn't fooled. He could tell her heart wasn't in it. Maybe it was the steely look she sent him.

"Good," he said, stepping forward. "Bill and I were thinking steak. Any objections?"

"I'm not dressed for a nice restaurant," Elise objected, raising her chin.

Bill responded, "We were thinking about that Australian place, Elise. It's casual, but the steaks are really good." He looked anxious. "But if you don't like that suggestion, we'll go somewhere else."

James was glad he hadn't said anything when he saw Elise's gaze soften.

She said to Bill, "No, Bill, that's fine. I love their food."

"Oh, good," he said with relief. "Frannie said she liked it, too."

James figured Frannie would have agreed to anything, even sushi, if Bill had suggested it. He'd like to see even half that much enthusiasm from Elise for being with him.

Funny how Bill couldn't see what was so obvious to James. Did Bill see Elise more clearly than he did? He'd admit his view was probably clouded by emotions. Not love. Sure, he liked Elise, but that didn't mean he wanted a commitment.

"Well, let's be on our way. We'll take separate cars so—"

"No," Elise contradicted James. "I'd like to visit with Frannie. I think we should all go together."

Bill looked at him.

Frannie looked at him.

Elise glared at him.

James knew when to back off. "Okay, that'll be fine. Shall I drive?"

"Let's take my car," Bill said. "I think the back seat is pretty roomy."

Bill was right, James decided once they were on their way. Bill drove a big SUV. "Do you do a lot of camping, fishing, Bill?"

"Yeah," Bill said from the front seat. "And some hunting, skiing. That's the great thing about living here in Arizona. There's lots to do."

"I like the outdoors," Frannie said, waving her hand at Bill.

James looked at the long nails, meticulously polished, the numerous rings on her fingers, the intricate hairdo, the wild clothes she wore—she was definitely not his type.

Bill, on the other hand, was staring at Frannie, obviously stunned by her statement. "You do?"

"Bill, the road," Elise called out.

Bill had drifted from his lane while he stared at Frannie.

"Oh, sorry. Good thing we're here, huh?" He found a parking space for his big vehicle.

"Looks crowded," Elise pointed out.

"Yeah, but it will give us more time to visit."

Frannie and Bill seemed to appreciate James's take on the situation, but Elise didn't.

Not that she said anything. But she turned to look out the window.

When Bill turned off the motor, James got out and hurried to Elise's door—the one she'd clung to during the ride—to help her out. But she was fast, and already standing on the sidewalk.

Bill helped Frannie out. As Frannie stepped to the

sidewalk, Elise caught her arm and started walking toward the entrance to the restaurant.

"Frannie, I don't think I told you, but that color looks good on you. Not too many women can wear it. When did you buy that blouse?"

Bill looked at James, but James only shrugged. The only subject he figured Frannie was interested in other than Bill was fashion. Elise was smart enough to use it to her advantage.

Elise had been right; the restaurant was crowded. Even the waiting area was crowded. Elise and Frannie stopped near a television showing a hockey game.

A loud television.

Elise was doing everything she could to avoid any conversation with James.

James was determined to outmaneuver her. He slid between her and the wall and whispered in her ear, "You're making it hard for Frannie to make any progress."

Rather than answer him, she shifted, stepping on his foot in the process. He didn't think it was an accident.

"Bill, do you follow the Coyotes?" Elise asked.

Since Bill was staring at Phoenix's hockey team play on the television, that was a safe question.

"Yeah, I'd forgotten the game was on tonight or I—I mean, I would've recorded it."

"Me, too. I hate to miss a game," Frannie said hurriedly. "I just love it when they hit a home run."

James covered his mouth and pretended to cough.

Elise tried to help her friend. "I think you mean a hat trick, Frannie."

"They do tricks, too? With a hat? I haven't seen that," Frannie said, staring intently at the television, obviously waiting for the players to show her a trick.

James was afraid Bill would have no patience with Frannie's lies, but much to his amusement, Bill smiled and put his arm around Frannie's shoulders. "Let me explain what Elise meant," he said. Then he dropped his voice, speaking only to Frannie.

"Nice job," James said, moving closer to Elise again.

"I didn't— Yes, at least *someone* is happy."

"Elise," he began with a sigh, "look, I admit I tricked you tonight, but your statement Wednesday night didn't leave me much choice."

"How typical of a man!" she snapped in a low voice. "You do what you want and then blame the woman!"

He wanted to retort that he'd done no such thing, but when put like that, he couldn't deny it. Frowning, he leaned closer, drawing in her scent even as he said, "You're right. That was wrong of me. Do you want to go home now?"

"And be condemned by everyone in Mesa Blue because I ruined Frannie's first date with Bill? I don't think so." She turned her back on him.

James really hadn't given a lot of thought to Elise's neighbors and what they'd think of his antics. He'd been amused by the star-crossed lovers, but he hadn't thought beyond that amusement.

Now he was *really* feeling guilty.

ELISE WAS SURPRISED that her words had had an effect on James. But they obviously had. He went to the bar and got them all glasses of iced tea. Then he struck up a conversation about the hockey game with the man standing next to him.

Leaving Elise alone.

Of course, she was glad. She'd wanted him not to bother her. Hadn't she? But she felt abandoned. Bill and Frannie were having a private discussion. James was talking to that man. She had no one to talk to.

By the time the hostess called them to their table, Elise was quite irritated.

Once they'd settled, she turned to Frannie, who was sitting on the other side of the booth with Bill. "Did you learn a lot about hockey?"

Frannie beamed at her. "Yes, so much. And Bill has promised to take me to a hockey game and explain everything to me."

"How nice," Elise said, surprised but pleased at how well things were turning out for Frannie.

"They're playing Tuesday here in Phoenix," James said.

"You follow them?" Bill asked.

"Yeah. The games are fun to go to. I'll get you tickets for the Tuesday night game if you can make it," he offered.

"You and Elise are going?" Frannie asked, leaning forward, excitement on her face.

"Uh, no," James said.

Elise was surprised. She'd seen him look at her first before he answered Frannie. She'd expected him to use the game to force her to go out with him again.

"Hey, man, we can't take tickets from you if you're not going to get to go. That would be cruel," Bill said.

"You wouldn't be taking my tickets. I have four," James said hurriedly.

"Then we could all go!" Frannie exclaimed.

James shook his head. "No, I can't make it."

"Oh," Frannie said, disappointment in her voice. Slowly, she said, "I guess we can't—"

"No, but I'll get us some seats, Frannie," Bill said, seemingly as interested in going as Frannie was. "Maybe a scalper—or I'll check the ads in the newspaper."

Which made Elise feel terrible. The Coyotes had been a great success in Phoenix. She knew all their games were sold out in advance. Somehow, she couldn't let Bill and Frannie down. "It's too bad you can't make it, James. I'd love to go to a game. I've watched it on television, but I've never seen a game in person."

James gave her a sharp look. With a frown, he said slowly, "I might be able to cancel my plans, if you're *sure* that's what you want."

Elise knew what he was doing. He was giving her plenty of opportunity to avoid going out with him. Her words had bothered him and he didn't want to be blamed for forcing another date.

But she couldn't ruin things for Frannie. Besides, as long as they were with the other couple, things would be all right.

"I'd like that," she said, looking at him.

The smile that lit his eyes almost had her retracting her words. Suddenly she wanted to fall into his arms. She'd pleased him. It was a heady experience.

"Done! They're great seats, right on the ice."

Suddenly, Elise asked. "Aren't those expensive

seats, almost impossible to get?'' Why would he have seats like that?

"Well," he said, pausing to swallow, "I didn't mean to mislead you. The seats actually belong to a friend. He has an ad agency and he uses the seats to entertain clients. But he gives them to me if he doesn't have any need for them."

"You sure they're free Tuesday night?" Bill asked. "Maybe you'd better check and let us know."

"Uh, right, I'll do that, but he's out of town next week, so I think we can definitely plan on going."

There was something about James's story that bothered Elise, but she couldn't think what it was. It was certainly plausible. She knew corporations bought season tickets to most sporting events and used them to entertain.

The waitress came to take their order.

When she'd left, Frannie said, "Bill knows about all the different sports. He said he could teach me all about them. Baseball, football, basketball." She snuggled against Bill's broad shoulders. "He's so patient with me."

"Baseball?" Elise asked before she stopped to think. But she'd watched baseball games with Frannie and knew she was a fan.

"Yes, Elise," Frannie said, frowning at her. "Do you want him to teach you about baseball, too?"

Well, I guess I'm slow, Elise decided. Frannie had faked her lack of knowledge about the hockey game to give Bill the chance to show off *his* knowledge. That was a dating rule that had been handed down mother to daughter for generations. It wasn't in the book she'd bought.

"Uh, thanks, but I happen to be a baseball fan."

"You are?" James asked. "Me, too." Then, after a look at Frannie that told Elise he'd figured out her pretense, too, he asked, "Who's your favorite player?"

He didn't believe her. She raised her eyebrows, letting him know she could read his mind. "Well, of course, Randy Johnson is such a dominating pitcher, any fan would name him, but I enjoy Jay Bell. He plays second base."

She'd pleased him again. That warm smile was her reward for being honest. Frannie's plan worked for her, but Elise was glad she'd followed the advice in *2001 WAYS TO WED*. Be honest with a man. If he doesn't like who you are, you don't want him, anyway.

Not that she wanted James!

He was still smiling at her, and she repeated that mantra to herself several times.

"We'll have to take in a baseball game, too," he said. He put his arm on the back of the booth, dropping his hand to her far shoulder.

She caught her breath. She hadn't intended for him to touch her. Her body went into overdrive with absolutely no warning.

"Uh, that would be fun, but there probably won't be time before we go to the wedding." She didn't get that warm smile again, but then she hadn't expected it. He knew by her answer that they wouldn't be going to a baseball game together. Because once they'd survived the wedding, she'd tell everyone he was in Hollywood.

He withdrew his arm. "Right."

"They're just getting started, anyway," Bill said, as if to console. "It'll be more fun when they get a few games under their belt. When's the wedding?"

"Next weekend, actually. It's gotten here faster than I thought it would, I've been so busy."

"Which church are they using?" Frannie asked. "My friend was married in this Episcopal church a few blocks away and it was a beautiful ceremony."

"They're getting married in Flagstaff."

Bill smiled. "Good thing it's your sister's wedding, or you might not drive that far. Does she live there?"

"No. She and her fiancé met on a ski trip there. They thought it would be romantic to marry at the place they first laid eyes on each other."

"On the ski slopes?" Frannie asked.

She could feel James's gaze on her. They hadn't discussed the wedding, even though it was the reason for their being together. "No. There's a historic church in Flagstaff. My sister's fiancé's father got permission for them to use it. We're all going up for three days to prepare for the wedding and have the rehearsal dinner."

"Three days," James murmured. "It'll be a mini-vacation. I'm looking forward to it."

She didn't look to see if he was smiling. She didn't want to know. "Good."

"You're going?" Frannie asked. "Together?"

Elise couldn't think of what to say.

James, however, could. "Yeah, I'm going with Elise. She mentioned it to me just after we met. You know, it's difficult to go to something like that without an escort. Now I'm glad she did. Maybe it will put her in a romantic mood.''

Elise glared at him. She didn't like his explanation. It made her sound—sound like an old maid, trying to hide the fact that no one wanted her.

Which, of course, was the truth.

Oh, not that no one wanted her, but she didn't want them.

She'd already found a man who lit her spark—he just happened to be all wrong for her. Figured!

Damn, was she becoming as romantic as Daisy?

Chapter Eleven

James called Elise after he got home. After all, it was only a few minutes past ten. She'd made sure there was no lengthy leave-taking.

In fact, she'd struck up another conversation with Frannie as they exited Bill's car, and maintained it until they reached Mesa Blue's front door. Then she'd told them all good-night and raced up the stairs as if a Doberman were after her.

James smiled ruefully as he pictured Bill and Frannie's expressions. After they'd recovered from the shock, they'd sent sympathetic looks his way.

Definitely feeling like a fifth wheel, he'd thanked them for their cooperation, promised to call them about Tuesday and headed for his car. *Someone* should have a sweet ending to the evening. He hoped Bill took advantage of their privacy.

"Hello?" she answered now.

"Elise, it's James. I didn't get a chance to tell you good-night earlier, so I thought I'd tell you now."

She didn't say anything. He guessed he couldn't blame her. It was a corny reason to call.

"Uh, good night," she finally muttered.

"Wait!" he called, afraid she'd hang up. "I had a question about the wedding."

"Yes?"

"When will we go up to Flagstaff?"

"I'm sorry, I should've informed you earlier. We'll leave as soon as you're free on Thursday."

"Do I need to book a room? What hotel—"

"No. My sister has made reservations for us at the Hilton in Flagstaff. It's very nice."

"I'm sure we'll be comfortable." After that polite response, he asked, "What shall I bring as a wedding present?"

"Nothing, James. You haven't even met them. You're coming as my escort. Sharon won't expect anything."

"But—"

"I'll get something from both of us, okay?"

She sounded frustrated. James wanted to soothe her. In fact, soothing her—and various *other* ways to make her happy—had been on his mind for several days.

"Sorry, Elise. I wasn't trying to create problems. And if you want to back out of Tuesday, it's all right."

She sighed. "I know you weren't. I'm sorry I'm so difficult right now. All this pretense—and I know it's all my fault, so don't say it, but—but I don't like it."

He didn't, either. He wanted to sweep Elise up into his arms and make love to her for at least a week. Instead, so he wouldn't scare her off, he had to pretend that touching her didn't affect him. Ha!

He cleared his throat. "And Tuesday?"

Holding his breath, he waited for her to answer. He wanted Tuesday night. That would give him another chance to get to know her before the wedding. That was the only reason it mattered, of course.

"If you don't mind, I think we should go ahead with Tuesday night. I think Frannie has found a way to connect with Bill. She'll go through all the sports. By that time, if he hasn't gotten the idea, it's hopeless, anyway."

"Was I wrong in thinking she knows more than she's letting on?"

Another sigh. "Women have done that for years, James, so don't condemn her."

"I wasn't. I was just curious."

"I'm not sure about hockey, but I do know that she's a baseball fan."

James remembered the pleasure he'd felt to discover that he and Elise shared a common interest in baseball. He nudged the conversation in that direction. For at least ten minutes, Elise relaxed and exchanged views about the Phoenix Diamondbacks and their competitors.

James was stretched out on his bed, imagining Elise next to him, sharing pillow talk, even if it was about baseball. It couldn't get much better than this—unless she were actually with him.

"Oh, James, I'm sorry, I didn't mean to rant and rave. You must be tired," Elise said.

He could hear in her voice the intent to hang up.

"No! I was enjoying your opinion." Deciding baseball was no longer a good discussion subject, he switched to movies. "I wanted to ask you about a new movie coming out. Some friends said it was good, but I'm not sure it would be worth the money.'' *Unless you're with me.*

Maybe he could convince her to continue their charade for the summer. He'd had more fun in the past week and a half than he'd had in years. That was it! He'd tell her it would be better if her family thought she was engaged for several months. Then when they broke it off just before their fake wedding date, she could pretend to be heartbroken for several years.

That would work.

Unless *he* was heartbroken.

Couldn't happen, he hurriedly reassured himself. But she was a fun companion. He enjoyed talking with her, having her beside him, discussing the twists and turns of life.

When they'd finished discussing the movie, he asked about Daisy's love life.

''I don't think we're making a lot of progress. She's going out with Dave tomorrow night, but she's not enthusiastic.''

''What about Phoebe's research at the gallery? Did she find anyone?''

''You were right. Several men tried to hit on her before she could explain about Daisy. And she found one guy she thought would do, but it turns out Daisy already knows him and refused to even consider him.''

''It's not easy to find someone who…a match. Find a match, I mean.''

''Do you believe there's only one person in the world for each of us?''

"No, definitely not. I think we may be predisposed toward a certain type."

"Was your wife your type?" she asked softly.

James swallowed. He hoped she wasn't. He'd hate to think he'd make that mistake again. If shallow, selfish women were his type, he'd definitely remain monastic.

"No," he said firmly. "I was young and idealistic. I didn't realize what kind of woman Sylvia was."

"So it was all her fault?"

"No, sweetheart, it's never all one person's fault. But I wasn't the right person for Sylvia, either. We were a bad combination. Like you and that Richard."

"I don't want to talk about romance anymore."

"Okay, let's talk about your career."

And they did. Among many things. James enjoyed the conversation. It was Elise who finally put an end to it.

"I really have to go. It's after eleven o'clock. I didn't mean to keep you on the phone so long."

"You didn't. I've enjoyed myself. What do you have planned for the weekend?"

Silence.

Then Elise said, "James, I don't think it would be a good idea for us to—I'll see you Tuesday evening, if you can get the tickets."

He'd known better than to try, but he hadn't been able to resist, especially after they'd talked so comfortably for so long.

"Okay. I'll check on the tickets and call you on Sunday."

"Or you could just call Bill. I'm sure he'd pass on the news."

"No, I'll call you."

They said good-night, and he reluctantly hung up the phone. He hadn't wanted to let her go.

At least he felt relieved that he and Sylvia hadn't had that kind of conversation in the six years they'd been married. Which meant his relationship with Elise was different. In fact, his marriage had gone more smoothly the *less* they'd talked.

With Elise, he could've talked all night.

Or found an alternative activity, if she'd been interested.

SATURDAY NIGHT at The Prickly Pear.

Phoebe and Elise sat together at their favorite table, dining on their favorite meal, served by their favorite waiter.

Neither of them was happy.

"Well," Elise began, then stopped.

"Yes?" Phoebe asked, but she didn't show much interest.

"Nothing."

Phoebe grimaced. "Why do we have the blues?"

Elise knew why she was unhappy, but she really didn't want to share the reason with Phoebe, or anyone for that matter. It might require that she admit something she didn't want to admit even to herself.

"Is everything all right at school?" she asked.

Phoebe looked around before she answered. "Not so loud. Remember, not many people know I'm in school."

"I don't think you should be so secretive about it, Phoebe. I'm proud of you for pursuing a degree."

"Yes, but you're female. Men don't… They think I'm too stupid and it's a waste of my time."

"So ignore them."

"I want to, Elise. I'm trying to. But my mother… Never mind, we've been over this before."

They had. Elise knew how Phoebe's mother had convinced her that her only asset was her looks. For a beautiful, brilliant woman, Phoebe didn't value herself very highly.

Phoebe interrupted her thoughts. "Everything's fine at school. I'm having a little trouble juggling my schedule at the spa, but I'll work it out."

"So if school or work isn't making you blue, what is?"

Phoebe shrugged. "I want Daisy to be happy but…I'll miss her."

Elise sighed. "I know. Things will be different if—*when* she marries and has a child. I know we'll still be friends but—"

"But there'll just be two of us hanging out here."

"Yeah."

"Maybe only one, if James has anything to say about it," Phoebe added, staring at Elise.

"Don't be ridiculous! You know the situation. When—when Sharon's wedding is over, James will go back to Sandra and I'll concentrate on my career again. I feel I've neglected it the past few days."

"Will you miss him?"

Elise hated that question. It was too close to the pain she was holding at bay. Too close to the truth she didn't want to admit.

"He's an interesting person. Just think, Phoebe, when he goes to Hollywood and becomes a star, we'll be able to say we knew him when." Hopefully that idea would distract Phoebe.

"You'll even be able to say you were engaged to him," Phoebe said. "Get him to give you a keepsake or something, autographed. Then, when he's famous, you can sell it. Or better yet, you can write a confessional book about how he stole your heart and then abandoned you for fame and fortune in Hollywood."

"All the while protesting how young and innocent I was?" Elise suggested, grinning. "I don't think I'd be believed."

"Not that you'd do it, anyway, even if it were true. That's more my mother's type of behavior."

Elise smiled. "Don't be too hard on her. We all have dreams that—well, we weren't all taught that hard work is the best way."

"I know." Phoebe propped her chin on her hand and sighed. "I think they need to write a book about 2001 ways to grow up. I could've used it when I was a kid."

Before Elise could agree, Phoebe waved at some new arrivals.

Elise's heart thumped in her chest as she spun around. She hated to admit how much she'd hoped it was James. Instead, Rolland and Helen Madison were making their way toward them. It was rare for them to eat out.

"Helen, Rolland, what are you doing here?" Phoebe asked.

"We felt like an evening out, dear. Are you waiting for some young men to join you?" Helen asked. "We don't want to interfere with your plans."

Phoebe and Elise denied having plans and asked the couple to join them.

"We were feeling lonesome because Daisy isn't here this evening, so we'd appreciate the company," Phoebe added.

"Where is she?" Rolland asked.

Phoebe and Elise exchanged a look. They hadn't told the Madisons about their search for a man for Daisy because they knew the couple would immediately recommend their grandson Wyatt.

"She has a date tonight," Elise said, keeping her voice casual.

"Oh? Someone as nice as your James?" Helen asked, beaming at Elise.

"Well, of course, I don't think so—but he's a professor at the university. He's a nice man."

"Good for her," Rolland immediately said. "Helen and I often say we don't know what's wrong with the men of today that you three aren't married. It just doesn't seem right."

"But we don't have to worry about you, Elise, dear. After all, you've found James." After saying that, Helen picked up the menu and asked what she should order.

Elise much preferred discussing food to talking about James and their future together. She heartily recommended the chicken Caesar salad.

Rolland asked Phoebe about her classes. Though Phoebe didn't tell just anyone about her classes, she'd told the Madisons, asking them not to mention it to anyone else. Elise thought it was a good thing for Phoebe.

"Oh! We forgot to tell you our exciting news!"

Helen burst out, after George had taken their order and departed.

"What exciting news?" Elise asked, glad to have the conversation turned on the Madisons rather than herself.

"Wyatt's going to come see us!" Helen absolutely beamed, clapping her hands together.

"That's wonderful, Helen," Phoebe said, smiling, though she quickly exchanged a look with Elise.

"Now, Helen, you're jumping the gun," Rolland cautioned. "He said he'd *try* to get away."

"I'm sure he will this time, Rolland, honey. He hasn't been to see us in so long."

"He does seem to be a little lax about visiting," Phoebe agreed.

A mild statement, Elise thought, knowing Phoebe's feelings about what she termed Wyatt's neglect of his grandparents.

Helen protested. "Phoebe, dear, Wyatt's a very busy man. Besides, he was here in January, the weekend you three went skiing near Flagstaff. We were so disappointed you missed meeting him."

"Yes, of course, I'd forgotten that trip. And we were sorry, too," Phoebe said.

Elise hid her smile. The three of them had even discussed the possibility that Wyatt was a fictitious character, made up by Rolland and Helen to satisfy their need for family.

Rolland leaned forward. "The boy's even talking about moving to Phoenix."

"Moving to Phoenix?" Phoebe asked faintly.

"Nothing's decided, but he wants to," Helen assured them, her smile even broader. "Wouldn't that be wonderful?"

"Yes, wonderful," Elise murmured.

"We've told him about you three. We've even hinted, delicately, of course, that you'd all three be wonderful candidates for his wife. We want Wyatt to marry and settle down."

This time when Elise and Phoebe exchanged a look, they each saw panic in the other's eyes.

"Oh, no, I'm not interested in marriage," Elise hurriedly said.

"I can't— I have plans for a career," Phoebe added.

"Well, how about Daisy? I heard her say she wants to marry and have a family," Helen suggested, though she looked disappointed at their protests.

"Daisy does want to marry," Elise said hesitantly, not wanting to sic Wyatt on her friend without talking to her first. "But you never know. She may fall in love with Dave, the professor she's with tonight."

Helen actually seemed upset, and Rolland reached out to take her hand in his.

Elise's heart ached at his tenderness. Over fifty years together, and he still cared about his wife's happiness. Still loved her. Elise wondered if that kind of love was even possible in today's world.

"There's Daisy, now," Phoebe pointed out.

Elise whirled around. "Is she alone?"

Phoebe grimaced. "I'm afraid so."

Daisy joined them, pulling up an extra chair. "Hi, guys. I was hoping you'd still be here," she said with a smile that didn't reach her eyes.

Elise didn't bother asking how the date had gone.

It wasn't difficult to tell that it had been a bust. And she didn't think Daisy would want to tell them the details in front of Rolland and Helen.

"We got a late start and just got here a few minutes ago," Phoebe told her. "Have you eaten? Rolland and Helen just put in their order so—"

"No, I don't want anything to eat. I'll get a cup of coffee when George comes by," Daisy said.

Helen had to repeat her announcement about her grandson for Daisy, watching her like a little bird looking for its first worm of the day.

"That's nice," Daisy said with a patient smile, but no enthusiasm.

Rolland changed the subject.

Not five minutes later, Frannie found them and asked to join them for dinner. Of course, they agreed. Helen hadn't heard anything about Frannie's date with Bill and wanted all the details.

Elise noted that Frannie sat so she could see the door. Elise knew who she was looking for.

She shouldn't be so obvious, Elise told herself. That's why *Elise's* back was to the door. And because James wasn't coming. She'd made it clear she didn't want to see him until Tuesday night.

So she shouldn't have hoped he'd come when Phoebe waved to Rolland and Helen. And she shouldn't still be hoping. Hoping he'd come, he'd call, he'd— She sighed.

"You all right?" Rolland asked, leaning toward Elise, a caring look on his face.

She gave him a quiet smile. "I'm fine. And Rolland, Helen is a lucky woman to have you."

"Well, Elise, it's kind of you to say that, but it

took her a lot of hard work and long years to train me properly. Don't give up on these young men. Your James seems eminently trainable to me.''

She gave a shaky smile. ''Maybe I'm the problem. I don't think I have Helen's talents.''

''You've got more talent than you realize. Trust your heart, young lady. That's all you've got to do.''

She wished life were that simple. Her heart wanted James. But he was all wrong for her. An actor, younger than her, involved with another woman. Even if she wanted to commit herself to marriage— and she didn't, she hurriedly told herself—she couldn't find that happiness with James.

If she gave in to the lust that filled her, she felt sure she'd be sated, satisfied, by James's lovemaking. But she'd be emptier than ever when he moved on.

She'd have her career, she stoutly assured herself. She enjoyed her students. She loved the French language. Just because her students left her, year after year, didn't mean she wasn't doing something meaningful with her life.

That pep talk got her nowhere. She wanted to find a phone and call James.

''Oh, look! There's Bill!'' Frannie exclaimed, the look on her face telling everyone how excited she was to see him. Then her expression collapsed and she subsided in her chair, her half-raised hand falling to the table. ''He—he's with a woman.''

Everyone at the table turned to stare, as Bill escorted his companion to a table on the other side of the room, his hand solicitously at her back.

''Nice-looking woman,'' Rolland said with approval, until small, delicate Helen elbowed him in his ribs. "Uh, I mean, I, uh, I think George is bringing our meal."

Fortunately for Rolland, he was right, and the delivery of their meals distracted everyone for a few minutes. Except Frannie. She gave George her order, but it was obvious her heart wasn't in it.

It was painful the rest of the evening to see Frannie's heartbreak. She picked at her food and seldom spoke.

Elise reminded herself *she* certainly wasn't going to wear her heart on her sleeve. Besides, she wasn't really in love with James the way Frannie seemed to be with Bill.

Jeff, on break from his bartending, strolled over to their table. "Well, well, looks like most of the gang's here." Then, as if he took count, he added, "Where's Bill?"

Frannie burst into tears and ran to the ladies' room.

Chapter Twelve

MaryBelle frequently watched television in James's den instead of her own sitting room because she loved his big-screen television. Once he'd offered to buy her one, but she'd flatly refused. Later she'd told him she'd assumed he'd offered because he didn't want her invading his space. It had taken him months to talk her back into his den.

Saturday night they were watching an NBA basketball game between the Phoenix Suns, the local team and the Chicago Bulls. It made him think of Frannie and her plan to ensnare Bill. Which, of course, made him think of Elise.

Did she like basketball? He had front-row seats for the Suns' home games, too. Maybe he should have offered— No, she wouldn't agree to that. Unless he could talk her into a longer...pretense.

"Why are you squirming so?" MaryBelle asked.

"I'm not," he assured her. Then he got up and headed for the kitchen. It was impossible to sit still.

MaryBelle followed him. "You should've said you were hungry. I'll fix you a snack. After all, you hardly touched your dinner."

"I'm not hungry. I just wanted to—to get a drink of water."

"Are you sure? I think you're losing weight."

It was tempting to tell his housekeeper that he already had a mother and didn't need another one, but he couldn't do that. "I'm fine. Just a little restless."

"Wondering what your lady is doing on Saturday night? I thought you'd take her out tonight."

"MaryBelle, you're fishing for information again," he pointed out, frowning at her.

"You bet I am. I promised Bobby I'd find out who she is."

"Well, you can just forget keeping that promise. I'm not telling you anything." He walked to the refrigerator to get some cold water.

"Maybe she's got another boyfriend. Could be she's out with him tonight."

He could feel her gaze fixed on him. "Nope. I don't think so."

"But you're not sure. You could call her," MaryBelle suggested.

His spirits leaped at the suggestion, but he'd told Elise he'd call Sunday. He didn't want her to think he was anxious. But he'd better get away from MaryBelle before she tempted him to do something foolish.

"I'm going up to my room. I've got some proposals for ad campaigns to review. See you in the morning."

Once he was secluded in his bedroom, he was even more restless. He prowled the room, staring at the walls as if he hadn't seen them before. Would Elise like it? He'd bought the house after his divorce, when his hard work had paid off and he'd had plenty of money. His mother had helped him pick out some things, but he'd made most of the choices himself.

He was being foolish. When would Elise see his bedroom? *Never.* She couldn't see it because she'd know he couldn't afford the house on Bobby's salary.

Besides, she didn't want that kind of involvement. That much she'd definitely made clear. But he was sure she'd enjoyed their conversation last night as much as he had.

He stared at the telephone on his bedside table. He even took a step toward it. Then he looked at his watch. It was just barely nine o'clock. He didn't want her to think he was checking on her.

Maybe she was spending the evening alone and would welcome a phone call. He could just call and see if she was busy. If she was, he'd hang up at once. Not bug her.

But it wouldn't hurt to see.

Before he could talk himself out of it, he reached for the phone and dialed Elise's number.

"Hello?"

"Elise, it's James. Is this a bad time?"

"Uh, sort of."

His heart sank. "Sorry, I didn't think about you having company this time of— That is, I'll call tomorrow as I said."

"Uh, James, if it's about Tuesday night, I don't think we can—"

"What about Bill and Frannie's romance?" he asked hurriedly. He didn't want her to cancel Tuesday night.

"That's the problem. Frannie is here and—and she's a little upset with Bill." Elise's voice had lowered, as if she didn't want anyone to hear her.

"What happened?" he asked. He wanted to know, of course, but he was also relieved that it was Frannie distracting her and not another man.

"Just a minute. I'm going to change phones."

Then he heard her ask Daisy to hang up the phone when she picked up in the bedroom.

"Are you still there?" she asked a few seconds later.

They both heard the *click* as Daisy hung up the receiver in the other room.

"Yeah."

Elise didn't waste any time. "Frannie was with us at The Prickly Pear when Bill came in with another woman."

"Who was she?"

"We don't know, but Frannie is distraught."

"Isn't she jumping to conclusions?" he asked, thinking maybe Frannie had overreacted.

"You don't understand. Frannie was married before, but her husband was very controlling. He didn't want her to have nice clothes, to wear anything bright, to use makeup. And he never took her out. Then she discovered he was paying for a mistress to enjoy all the things he was keeping from her. That's why she dresses like she does. She was so hurt. Now, if a man even looks at another woman, she won't have anything to do with him. For Bill to— Well, it's broken her heart."

"Poor thing. I wish there was something I could do."

"There's not anything. It's Bill's business."

"Yeah."

"Anyway, I have to go, but don't bother about the tickets Tuesday night. Thanks, anyway."

After she hung up, James sat on the edge of his bed, trying to think through what had happened. He didn't want to give up their date to the hockey game. Could he talk Elise into going without them?

Probably not. Too bad Bill and Frannie were having problems. They seemed perfect for each other.

So why hadn't anyone asked Bill? Elise had said it was his business, but James didn't think Bill was the kind of man who would two-time a woman. True, he and Frannie weren't committed, but still...

He considered calling Bill. Then he checked his watch. Nope. He would go over to visit him. He could tell Bill he was in the area.

James grabbed the keys to MaryBelle's car and ran down the stairs. He stopped in the den to tell her he was borrowing her car again. Then he headed for the back door before she could ask any questions.

In minutes, he was knocking on Bill's apartment door. It hadn't occurred to him until then that Bill might not be home. A lot of dates—though not any of *his* lately—lasted beyond nine-thirty.

Then Bill opened the door.

"James, come in. What are you doing here?"

"I stopped by earlier to see if you wanted to grab a bite, but you were out. So I ate dinner. But I came back by to talk about Tuesday night."

Bill looked disappointed. "You couldn't get the tickets? That's okay. I appreciate your asking."

"No, I have the tickets. Can you still make it?"

"Of course we can," Bill said, sounding enthused.

"Oh, good." Now what? Bill hadn't responded to his implied question about earlier. "Were you out with Frannie tonight?"

"Frannie? Gosh, no. We're going out Tuesday."

Right. Obviously Bill wasn't as intent on seeing Frannie as James was on seeing Elise.

"I was showing a condo to a nice lady. I only have the one vacancy, so I wasn't concerned, but I think she's going to take it."

"Oh, great. So, if you haven't eaten, I'll go with you and have a cup of coffee."

"Oh, we ate. She asked me to take her to a local restaurant, and we went to The Prickly Pear."

"Good place to eat. I like it."

Bill smiled in return but said nothing else.

"Shall we plan on dinner before the hockey game Tuesday?"

"I'd like that. Make an evening of it. I want Frannie to enjoy the experience," Bill said, his eyes lighting up. James changed his mind about Bill not being interested in seeing Frannie.

"Okay. Do you mind driving again? Your car is certainly bigger than mine."

"I'll be glad to. In fact, I'll buy dinner. After all, you're supplying the tickets."

James insisted they each treat the ladies, because the tickets weren't costing him anything. They parted then, Bill looking pleased about his visit.

James was ecstatic. Not only was he going to help Frannie and Bill, but he was also going to see Elise tonight. He hurried up the stairs and rapped on Elise's door.

ELISE, DAISY and Phoebe had been commiserating with Frannie for almost an hour. She'd stopped crying, eventually.

Now she was angry.

And planning revenge.

They'd pointed out to her that Bill hadn't made any promises, so it wasn't fair to treat him as if he'd betrayed her.

She'd carefully explained that after finally having her first date with him, after longing for that moment for several years, it was rotten of him to date someone else.

They all agreed with that, but they tried to move her away from the idea of running into his SUV, or shoving him down the stairs or burning down his apartment.

A knock interrupted them.

"Yes?" Elise asked as she approached the door.

"It's James." His strong masculine voice could be heard through the wood.

Elise was surprised. She'd hoped he'd call tomorrow, as he'd said—but to show up tonight? She opened the door and stepped through.

"Aren't you going to invite me in?" he complained.

Startled by that response, she looked up at him. Before she could answer, he kissed her.

It wasn't easy to back away from what she'd been longing for. But she did. Though not immediately. Breathlessly, she said, "James, what are you doing here?"

"I've come with information."

"About the tickets? I told you—"

"About Bill."

That response brought her up short. She studied his handsome face, noting the smile. "I hope you've got good news, because Frannie is turning violent."

"I think it is. Do I get to come in?"

"Of course," she said, opening the door wide.

He stepped over the threshold, his gaze scanning her living room. She wasn't too worried about his approval. She was happy with the decor. Phoebe, who was great with colors, and Daisy, with her artistic talents, had given Elise some suggestions, but she'd done most of it on her own. It suited her.

"Good evening," he said with a smile.

His audience, all three seated on the sofa, stared at him as if he'd lost his mind. Elise decided she should explain before Frannie started throwing things.

"James says he has some news about Bill."

That got their attention.

"I don't want to hear anything about that miserable excuse for a human being!" Frannie exclaimed.

Elise opened her mouth to protest, but James responded before she could.

"Are you sure, Frannie? Because Bill is still counting on Tuesday night. He said he wanted you to have a good time."

Frannie burst into tears again.

"Frannie, don't cry," Daisy pleaded. "Let James explain what he means." She smiled encouragingly to James, then frowned. "You do know about—" After a quick glance at Frannie, she mouthed the words *the other woman?*

James nodded. Then he turned to Elise. "I was

going to ask Bill to eat with me tonight, but he was tied up on business.''

Frannie made some kind of noise signifying disgust.

''Apparently there's an empty unit, and he showed it this evening to a lady who's thinking about taking it. She asked Bill to show her a place to eat, and he took her to The Prickly Pear.''

Phoebe looked at Frannie, then at James. ''So it wasn't a date.''

''He looked very happy,'' Frannie said, raising her head long enough to get the words out clearly before she buried her face back in her hands.

Phoebe raised an eyebrow. ''Of course he did. You know Bill likes to keep Mesa Blue fully occupied. It's his pride and joy.''

''She was very attractive,'' Frannie said with a sniff.

''Bill didn't mention that,'' James said.

Frannie wiped the tears from her face.

''You know how hard it is to get Bill to notice *any* woman,'' Elise pointed out. ''You've been working on him for several years. And she wasn't nearly as attractive as you, Frannie.''

''He'd never taken me out to dinner until Friday night, and that was only because you suggested it, James.'' Then Frannie clapped her hand over her mouth, her gaze darting to Elise.

James reassured her. ''Don't worry, Frannie. Elise had it all figured out before she even got downstairs. But she wanted you and Bill to have a good time. You're not going to refuse to go Tuesday night, are you?''

"You got the tickets?" Frannie asked.

James nodded.

"Well, then, I suppose I couldn't disappoint the three of you. If that woman thinks she's going to waltz in here and latch on to Bill, she's got another think coming." Frannie rose, squared her shoulders and marched to the door. There, she paused. "Thanks, girls, for comforting me. You're good friends. You, too, James. Oh, and let's not mention my little upset to Bill." Then she left.

Phoebe sagged back against the sofa. "James, I could kiss you."

"Me, too," Daisy agreed, "but I think Elise might protest."

Elise felt her cheeks turn red, and she looked anywhere but at James. "It was good of you to help us out," she said stiffly.

"My pleasure. We made such progress Friday night, I didn't want it to fall apart."

"You didn't tell Bill that Frannie was upset, did you?" Phoebe asked suddenly. "She'd be humiliated if he knew."

"No. I asked nosy questions, but I didn't mention that. He probably thinks I'm half crazy, but the hockey tickets kept him from throwing me out." He grinned at all three of them.

"Do you think he wants to go with Frannie?" Elise asked. "He might really be attracted to the other woman."

"Nope. He said he wants the hockey game to be a good experience for Frannie. That's why we're going to dinner first."

Elise frowned. That meant more time spent with James. She'd enjoy herself, but that worried her.

"We're going in Bill's car...together," James added, as if he knew she was worried.

She rewarded him with a smile. He deserved it. The smile he gave her in return made her want to melt into his arms.

Suddenly Phoebe and Daisy stood and were heading to the door. "We'll go now. I'm tired," Phoebe said, offering a yawn.

"Yeah, it's been a long day," Daisy added.

"But you haven't told us about your date with Dave," Elise protested, partly because she wondered what had happened and partly because she was afraid to be alone with James.

"Oh, suffice it to say, I won't be going out with Dave again." Daisy started out the door.

"Wait!" Elise called. "What did he do? He's always seemed nice enough."

"For an octopus. He's got more hands than any man I've ever dated. He couldn't understand my reluctance to have sex with him before we'd even eaten."

James stood, frowning. "He didn't hurt you?"

"No," Daisy protested, but her cheeks were flushed. "I'll admit he scared me a little. I didn't think he was going to stop...but he did."

"I'll talk to him," James said, his voice firm.

All three protested. Elise stepped closer to James. "Really, it's all right. Daisy is safe, and we like to take care of our own problems."

"Independent ladies? I understand, but if you need

me, Daisy, or you, too, Phoebe, I'll do what I can for you. Any friend of Elise is a friend of mine.''

Elise couldn't bring herself to mention the temporary nature of their relationship. She believed his words came from his heart, and they were very sweet. She could tell her friends thought so, too.

They both stepped forward to kiss James's cheek. Then they said good-night and slipped from the apartment.

''Well,'' she said with a sigh, clutching her hands in front of her to stop herself from reaching out to touch him, ''you've certainly played the role of Superman, saving the day, James. Thank you very much.''

He stepped to her side. ''I was glad to do it. But don't make me out to be too heroic. I used Frannie's problem as an excuse to see you tonight.'' He reached his hands out and ran them up and down her arms.

''But you were already here when you offered to protect Daisy and Phoebe,'' she pointed out.

''No woman should be treated like that.''

''I know. I feel badly that the man I set her up with did that. I've never heard any whispers about Dave. I thought he seemed like a nice man.'' Elise vowed to check out any prospective dates for Daisy a little more thoroughly in the future.

''Don't feel guilty. That's not something a woman would know,'' he assured her.

As he said those soft words, he wrapped his arms around her, gently tugging her against him.

It felt like coming home. Warm, exciting, comforting. She leaned against him, letting her head rest on his strong shoulder. His fingers sifted through her hair.

"I called because I couldn't stop thinking about you," he whispered.

Shivers rolled through Elise. "I hoped you would. But then I got distracted by Frannie. And I'd told you to stay away."

"I didn't want to," he assured her. He captured her chin and tilted her head up until his lips met hers.

Elise couldn't help giving in to his temptation. The man seemed to know every button to push.

The telephone rang.

Saved, she thought. Otherwise, she might've invited him into her bedroom.

"Hello?"

A feminine voice, a young woman, asked, "Is James there?"

Elise admitted to herself she'd needed a reminder of James's role in her life, but she hadn't expected one so soon. "Is this Sandra?"

"Why, yes!" the young woman exclaimed, startled.

"Just a moment." Elise held out the receiver to James. "It's for you."

Then she moved to stand beside the door, ready to escort him out of her apartment before he could convince her differently. As soon as he finished his conversation with Sandra.

Frowning, James took the phone. "Hello?"

Elise pretended not to listen. There wasn't much to listen to. Just an "Of course." "Yes." "Bye."

Then he came toward her.

She swung open the door.

"Good night."

"Elise, let me explain."

"That's quite all right. I hope she understood."

"A lot more than you do," he muttered.

If she got any stiffer, she feared she'd never move again. "I apologize if I'm not good at pretending."

"That's not what I meant. Elise, let me—"

"Please leave, James. I'll see you Tuesday night."

With a sigh, he walked past her.

Though she longed for a last kiss, she slammed the door after him before he could even turn around. She couldn't take that risk.

Besides, it wouldn't be fair to Sandra.

Even more, it wouldn't be fair to her. Just once, now that she was alone, she could admit that she'd done the one thing she'd promised herself she wouldn't do.

She'd fallen in love with James.

Chapter Thirteen

James drove directly from Elise's apartment to the Good Samaritan Hospital. Sandra had called because Bobby had broken his arm.

After making sure his brother was all right, James asked the question that had bothered him. "How did you get Elise's number? I didn't think you had it."

"It was on caller-ID. Remember, she called the apartment looking for you?" Bobby said.

James frowned. "You kept it?"

"I jotted it down. Never know when it might come in handy," Bobby assured him with a grin. Probably because James continued to frown, he asked, "It wasn't a problem, was it?"

James felt guilty complaining when his brother was sitting there in pain. Or, at least, he had been hurting until he took a pain pill. Now he seemed a little loopy. "No, of course not." He turned to the young woman who was unknowingly playing such an important role in his own life right now. "It was good of you to drive him to the hospital, Sandra."

"It was the least I could do," the young woman replied, looking guilty.

"Honey, I told you it wasn't your fault," Bobby protested. "We shouldn't have been wrestling."

James's eyebrow rose. "Wrestling? I should think not."

Sandra turned bright red. "We weren't really. I found a picture of Bobby when he was little and he didn't want me to see it."

James knew immediately which picture Sandra was talking about. Their mother had believed in taking crying pictures of her sons. It was hard to appear macho with tears streaking down your cheeks. "Oh. I see."

Bobby closed his eyes. "I should've burned it."

"I thought it was sweet," Sandra said, a dreamy smile on her face.

James had seen that look before on his brother's women. He only hoped Bobby felt the same way. "Look, I'll take Bobby back to my house. MaryBelle can fuss over him for a couple of days, until he's better. I don't think he should be alone while he's taking pain pills."

"I could take care of him," Sandra offered eagerly.

"You'll have to go to classes. But feel free to visit him at my house whenever you want. MaryBelle will love the company."

Once he'd seen Sandra on her way, James drove his car to the exit door and loaded Bobby in.

"Where's your spiffy Mercedes?" Bobby asked in slurred tones.

"At home. Are you okay?"

"Yeah. Just—sleepy." Then he put his head back and began to snore.

James reached for his car phone to warn Mary-Belle that they were having a guest, then realized he didn't have a phone in the borrowed car. He guessed Bobby would have to be a surprise.

Like the surprise he'd gotten when Sandra called Elise's apartment. Damn, he hadn't known how he'd explain that to Elise, even though he'd offered. He couldn't tell her his brother had broken his arm. She might see Bobby at school, once he was up and around, and, as much as they looked alike, Elise might put two and two together.

All this subterfuge was draining. He'd liked the anonymity he'd borrowed when he first assumed Bobby's identity, but now it was bothersome. Elise enjoyed his company without knowing about his money. That was good. But she also didn't want anything to do with him because she thought he was in love with Sandra.

He couldn't tell her it was Bobby who loved Sandra.

He was the one who loved Elise.

"No!" he exclaimed, almost driving off the road. He'd promised himself to never again be vulnerable to a woman. But Elise wasn't Sylvia. That much he knew.

The important thing was not to move too fast. Not to make a declaration until he was sure. Right now, he enjoyed Elise's company. He wasn't ready to commit to anything, he assured himself. Besides, there were too many roadblocks in the way right now.

But one thing was for sure, Elise sure made life fun again.

ELISE WORE HER JEANS Tuesday night. But she also wore a cotton sweater that more than covered her rear. While it was warm during the day in March, the evenings were in the low sixties. And sitting beside an ice rink for the game would be even cooler. She'd need the comfort of the long sleeves.

And the sweater wasn't green.

It was a teal blue that gave her eyes a blue cast. She pulled her hair back in a ponytail, though it wasn't as severe as she usually wore to school; several strands curled around her face. With gold hoops in her ears, she thought she'd achieved a casual, nonseductive appearance.

She wouldn't want James to know how long she'd spent choosing the perfect outfit.

Nor did she want James to know how long she'd grieved over Sandra's phone call. That he had given her number to his real girlfriend shouldn't have been a surprise. But it was.

Tonight, she intended to concentrate on hockey, not her escort. There would be no exchange of kisses.

Did he tell Sandra he'd kissed Elise?

Elise clenched her fists. If *her* boyfriend were kissing another woman, she'd murder him. Good thing James wasn't her boyfriend, because she suspected he was kissing Sandra.

The picture that had been in the newspaper popped into her head. Yes, he was definitely kissing her.

Fighting off the depression that filled her, she grabbed her shoulder bag and went down to Frannie's apartment. She didn't want any time alone with James.

Frannie definitely hadn't gone the casual, nonseductive approach in her choice of clothing. She wore a red short-sleeved, V-neck sweater that showed off every curve and offered a seductive view of her cleavage. The sweater ended at the top of her tight jeans. If she raised her arm, Elise knew, she'd be showing skin.

"Um, aren't you afraid you'll get cold?" she asked Frannie, after her friend had invited her into the apartment.

"I'm hoping," Frannie said with a big smile. "Then Bill will have to hold me close to keep me warm."

"Oh." Elise sat on the couch and reached for a cat.

"Didn't you learn anything at your mother's knee, child?" Frannie asked.

"I guess not." She looked at Frannie again. "So you've forgiven Bill? No anger left?"

"No. No anger. But I'm determined to show him what he's got to lose if he messes around with other women. What do you think of this new perfume?"

Elise sniffed and smiled at Frannie, even though she didn't much care for the scent. It was a heavy, musk-laden smell, probably seductive to men, but it did nothing to her. "It's unforgettable."

"That's what I thought. I'm prepared—"

Someone knocked and Frannie hurried to the door and swung it open. James stood there.

"Frannie, have you talked to Elise? I knocked on her apartment door, but there was no answer."

Frannie stepped back and swung the door wider. "She's here with me."

Elise should have been flattered by the relief visible on James's face, but she shut that thought out of her head. "Hello, James. I thought it would be easier if we all met here at Frannie's apartment."

James stared at her, and she could tell he didn't believe her excuse. Too bad.

"Is Bill here?" he asked, stepping into the apartment.

"Not yet. Sit down, James," Frannie suggested, "and I'll go see what's keeping him."

"No!" Elise protested, jumping to her feet. "I mean, there's no point in that. We'll go with you, Frannie, and then head straight for his car. We don't want to be late."

"Okay," Frannie agreed. "Come on, and I'll lock up after you."

Again Elise felt James's stare on her, but she wasn't going to let it bother her. As she stepped out into the hallway, she saw Bill. "Oh, there's Bill."

"Am I late?" Bill asked as he joined her and James.

"No," James assured him. "We were coming to check on you, though. Elise doesn't want to be late."

Bill was about to respond when he caught sight of Frannie. He visibly swallowed before he said, "Hi, Frannie. You look lovely tonight." He seemed to think about what he'd said because he added, "I mean, you both look lovely tonight. James and I are, uh, lucky to be your escorts."

Frannie gave him a flirtatious smile, linked her arm with his, and said, "You bet you are, sailor. Ready?"

They walked off, leaving James and Elise standing

alone. She immediately turned to hurry after them, but James caught her arm.

"Are you afraid to be alone with me, Elise?" he asked.

"Don't be silly. I just don't want to keep them waiting."

"Is that why you came downstairs to Frannie's apartment?"

"Why else would I come down?" she asked, staring at him, daring him to suggest anything else.

"You coming?" Bill asked as he held open the front door of Mesa Blue.

Left with no choice, James started moving, but he snagged Elise's hand and held on as she hurried toward Bill.

"Let me go," she whispered, trying to tug her hand away.

James ignored her.

She was able to keep her distance, thanks to Bill's bucket seats, until they were seated in the restaurant Bill had chosen. It was an Italian eatery with cozy booths. James followed her as she slid in, his arm going around her shoulders.

She shrugged, as discreetly as she could, to dislodge him, but he ignored her.

"After I saw all of you Saturday night, guess where I ended my evening," he said with a casual air, but Elise caught the look he sent her way.

"You saw Frannie and Elise Saturday night?" Bill asked, frowning.

"Oh, yeah, I stopped by Elise's apartment after I talked to you, and Frannie, Phoebe and Daisy were there. I guess they were having a hen party."

Frannie had tensed, but after his explanation, she visibly relaxed.

"Where?" she asked, smiling.

"The hospital emergency room. My—my roommate had an accident."

"You have a roommate?" Frannie asked. "Aren't you a little old to—I mean, it's none of my business, but—"

James's cheeks flamed. "When I started back to school, I had to cut down on expenses."

Elise would have felt bad about the expensive prices on the menu, but she reminded herself she'd pay in the long run when she settled up with James for his expenses.

Frannie sent a quick look at her escort. Then she said, "Look, we'll pay for the dinner this evening. After all, you got the tickets." Then, as if expecting Bill to object, she added, "I'll pay for our half, Bill."

James turned even redder, but Bill reached out to clasp Frannie's hand, which was resting on the table, and smiled sweetly at her. "I already offered, Frannie, but James insisted he pay his share. He said the tickets didn't cost him anything."

James leaned forward. "I can afford the meal, Frannie, but it's sweet of you to offer."

Frannie looked at Elise for advice, even as she clung to Bill's hand. "Elise?"

"I assure you, Frannie, James can afford the meal." Then she turned to him. "Is your roommate seriously injured?"

"No. But I've had to watch him. He's on pain pills."

"Ooh, I was on those once. I couldn't think

straight,'' Frannie exclaimed. She began telling an anecdote about her strange medication-induced behavior.

Elise pretended to listen attentively to Frannie's story, but she thought about James's tale. He was trying to explain why Sandra called. Was she dating his roommate? Or had she been waiting there for him to return?

What did it matter? She knew how Sandra felt about him. That picture had told it all. Even if he wasn't crazy about her—and thinking about the picture again, she didn't believe that—they had a relationship that was much more serious than what she and James shared.

Besides, Sandra wasn't paying for her relationship. Elise was.

She concentrated on the menu.

JAMES HAD HOPED that his carefully edited version of the truth would appease Elise, but he couldn't see much improvement in her demeanor. She avoided looking at him as much as possible and seldom spoke directly to him.

Plus, he'd thoroughly embarrassed himself by saying he had a roommate. He didn't want Elise to like him because he had money, but he didn't want anyone thinking he was so poor he couldn't pay his own way. He guessed his money and success meant more to him than he'd realized.

Which reminded him of his conversation with Elise's father. It was a relief that Sam knew James could, if he were really going to marry Elise, provide for her. He was glad he'd been able to tell Sam the truth, though. Sam had accepted the deception he was playing on Sam's daughter, as long as James promised not to do anything to hurt her.

He was trying.

When they reached the hockey arena, they found their seats. Several of the regular season-ticket holders spoke to him, which made Elise look at him sharply.

"I use the tickets a lot," he murmured to her as he waved to the others.

"I guess so. Everyone seems to know you."

Thank goodness he'd used his own name from the beginning, he thought with a sigh of relief.

"Ooh, this is so exciting!" Frannie enthused.

Bill nodded his head. "It's been a long time since I went to a live game. It's almost impossible to get tickets. These are great seats, James. You're lucky."

"Yeah, I am," James agreed. He'd taken his success and the benefits of it for granted the past couple of years. Had he turned into a prima donna? he wondered. With Elise beside him tonight, he was seeing things much more clearly.

About to speak to her, he was distracted by Frannie.

"Oh, my, I didn't realize how cold it would be next to the ice," she exclaimed, crossing her arms and shivering.

Bill frowned. "I should've told you to bring a light jacket. Here, I'll share—" He began stripping off the sports coat he was wearing.

"Oh, no, Bill, I can't let you do that. Then you'd be cold. If you just put your arm around my shoulders, I should be all right.'' She gave him a bright smile.

The man seated behind them leaned forward. ''If he don't want to do it, lady, I'll keep you warm.''

Frannie smiled at the man, but Bill glowered at him even as he wrapped an arm around Frannie. ''I think I can manage without any help.''

Frannie beamed at Bill and settled into his embrace. Then she looked at Elise and winked.

''What did that mean?'' James asked, whispering in Elise's ear.

He could tell she was thinking about ignoring him, so he wrapped his arm around her and pulled her closer.

She resisted, but she also answered his question in a whisper so as not to give Frannie away. ''She wore short sleeves for that reason.''

James wished Elise were as wickedly sneaky as Frannie. Instead, she was pulling away from him, pushing at his hand on her shoulder.

''Relax, Elise, I'm following Bill's example so he won't feel awkward.'' That was the best excuse he could come up with so he could hold Elise.

''*I'm* not cold.''

''You could pretend, couldn't you, for the sake of romance?''

She didn't say anything, since the crowd exploded as the Phoenix Coyotes took to the ice. Instead, she leaped to her feet, cheering, which effectively removed his hold on her.

The rest of the first period, Elise was up and down more than a jumping jack. Every time he put his arm around her, she found something to cheer about, until he heard one of the men behind her asking her why she kept jumping to her feet.

"I'm enthusiastic," she assured him with a smile.

James noted the effect of that smile on the man and ground his teeth. She wouldn't even look at him, much less smile, but she could melt that man's opposition with no problem.

"You'd better save that smile. It's a lethal weapon," he whispered as she sat back down.

"I don't know what you're talking about," she protested.

He leaned closer, loving the warm, sweet scent of her. "I'm talking about the smile you gave that guy. It's potent."

"You're being ridiculous," she said, and leaped to her feet again, as the goalie saved a puck drilled right at him.

After the period ended, he offered to go get popcorn and drinks, if anyone was interested. Both Bill and Frannie declined, but Elise asked for popcorn and a diet cola.

James suspected she'd asked for it to get rid of him for a while. But he had offered, after all. As he got up, Bill stood, too.

"I'll go with you," he said. "It'll give me a chance to stretch my legs."

FRANNIE WAITED until the men had disappeared, then leaned closer to Elise. "Are you and James still upset with each other? I thought you made up Friday night."

"We did," Elise assured her, "but I'm not sure

we're right for each other." She knew they weren't. If only she could convince her body.

"He seems awfully nice to me," Frannie said. "Of course, that could be because he's the reason Bill asked me out in the first place. You're not angry about me cooperating with him, are you?"

"Of course not. I know how long you've wanted to go out with Bill. I don't blame you in the least." Elise smiled at her friend. Frannie didn't have a mean bone in her body...unless Bill betrayed her.

At least Elise could understand those feelings. She'd wanted to break something, preferably over James's head, when she'd seen the picture of him and Sandra together.

The gentleman who'd offered to keep Frannie warm leaned forward to chat with her, and Elise sat back with a sigh. She enjoyed hockey, and seeing the game live was so different from watching it on television. But she was ready for the evening to end.

Suddenly, she realized James was the subject of Frannie's conversation. That got her attention.

"You friends with James?" the man asked Frannie.

"Yes, we are."

"No need to tell me she is," the man said with a snort of laughter, nodding toward Elise. "He don't usually bring a woman."

Frannie sent a beaming smile Elise's way, as if to say that her being there with James was significant. Instead, it probably meant Sandra didn't like hockey.

"Have you known him long?" Frannie asked.

"We've both been regulars for the past five years," he said. "I'm a hockey junkie. Can't stay away. I don't think he's as enthusiastic. Usually leaves early. Me, I stay to the bitter end.''

"That seems wasteful," Frannie said.

"Naw, it don't matter. These companies buy the tickets for business, anyway. When he brings a client, he stays to the end, too. But if not, he doesn't seem that interested.''

Elise looked at the man. ''A client? James brings clients?''

Her back was to the steps at the end of the row, so she wasn't aware James had returned until he answered her question.

"Sometimes I help out. Hey, Smitty, what do you think of the game so far?''

"It's a good one," the man said, "but not as good as the game you've got going.'' He nodded at Elise and grinned.

"Don't embarrass my—my lady friend," James said with a laugh. He handed Elise a bag of popcorn and her drink, and sat down beside her, letting Bill pass over to his seat.

"That was fast," she muttered. Now she was faced with eating the popcorn she didn't want.

"Short lines. Eat up, Elise. I know you must be starving.'' He shot her a teasing look that told her he knew she wasn't hungry.

Just to show him, she put a handful of popcorn in her mouth and chewed determinedly, ignoring his friendliness. She was trying to keep her heart as cold toward James as the ice in front of her.

But he was a master at melting it.

Chapter Fourteen

Elise approached Thursday with dread.

It wasn't her sister's wedding. Or the trip to Flagstaff. Or missing a day at the university. She'd arranged for one of her colleagues to cover her classes.

It was James.

She was torn apart by the fear of spending more time with him, and mourning the end of their whatever-they-had-going-on between them. Tuesday night she'd spent so much time trying to resist his charm that she'd scarcely been aware of the action on the ice.

Or the action beside them. Frannie appeared to have made inroads against Bill's resistance. They'd snuggled together, whispering to each other.

Elise didn't hang around at the end to see if all that closeness resulted in a sweet good-night, either. She had to escape James's presence as soon as possible.

The man was lethal!

They'd spoken briefly on the phone Wednesday night, setting a time for their departure. James had wanted to continue to chat, but Elise had claimed an emergency and hung up. It was pitiful when a man could draw such a response when she could neither see nor smell him, only hear his voice.

That deep, silky voice that inspired incredible dreams.

Now she was all packed, waiting for the last hurrah. Three days with James. Surrounded by her family.

It seemed to her that they should take her car because the drive to Flagstaff included long miles with no habitation in sight. If they broke down out there, it might take a while before any help arrived. Even with her cell phone.

James, however, said he'd already thought of that and had promised to provide a safe vehicle.

She also hoped he'd listened to the weather reports. Arizona had an amazing diversity of weather. Flagstaff was only two or three hours from Phoenix, yet it was mid-seventies in Phoenix today, but there was a cold front in Flagstaff that might bring snow. The ski area just north of Flagstaff was celebrating. Elise suspected her sister Sharon was not.

Mentally reviewing the contents of her suitcase, she was startled by the knock on her door. She checked her watch and realized it was probably James. Drawing a deep breath, she answered.

"Ready?" James asked, that warm smile of his firmly in place.

Why couldn't he be grumpy and disagreeable at least some of the time? He'd shown patience, concern, a sense of humor, interest, support... She could go on naming his good qualities forever. The only fault she'd found was his concealing his relationship with Sandra.

Of course, that was a major fault—one she couldn't forgive. Maybe she should be grateful for that fault because it kept her from making a fool of herself.

"Yes." She turned to pick up her suitcase, but James grabbed it first.

"I've got it." He lifted the bag, then cocked his eyebrow at her. "You packed heavy."

She avoided his eyes, those blue eyes with little smile lines. "There're a lot of changes needed for this event. And I brought warm clothes. Did you hear the weather report?"

"Yeah. Looks like we might have a little winter."

"Will your car—? I mean, it might snow on the way. Do you have good tires?"

"Yeah, brand-new ones. I borrowed a friend's new SUV. After riding in Bill's, I decided I like that kind of vehicle."

"Doesn't your friend mind? We'll be putting a lot of miles on it," she asked, walking to the stairs, carrying a coat over her arm.

"No, he won't mind," James assured her, his voice cheerful.

It seemed a bit excessive to borrow a friend's new car for such a trip, but she knew from experience that James could charm anyone into anything. And what a favor! With her first glimpse of the vehicle, she loved it. It was dark green, with silver-gray leather seats and every amenity one could wish for.

"Wow! This is incredible. And very expensive. I

hope you have good insurance in case anything happens.''

He laughed as he helped her in. ''Don't go wishing disasters on us, Elise. We'll be fine.''

Which didn't answer her question. What if she was responsible for any damages? She had a healthy savings account, but not enough to pay for one of these babies. But as James had said, she shouldn't borrow trouble.

Once they left Phoenix, the land was barren. Cacti-covered rolling hills led to small mountains, and signs indicated the altitude as the road began climbing.

''I haven't made this trip in a while,'' James said.

''Phoebe, Daisy and I went skiing outside Flagstaff in January for the weekend.''

''Sounds like fun. I haven't stopped to enjoy life in a while. Thanks to you, I'm doing that again.'' Another warm smile.

''Thanks to me? I haven't done anything,'' she protested.

He continued to smile but didn't argue with her. ''Maybe we can try skiing this weekend.''

She shook her head. ''I'm afraid my sister has the entire time mapped out for me. You may have some free time tomorrow morning while we have the bridal luncheon, if you want to go by yourself, but I won't be able to.''

''I assume we have the rehearsal dinner tomorrow night?''

''Yes. And one of my aunts is hosting a party this evening, right after we get there. It will be casual. Then the wedding is actually at eleven Saturday morning, followed by a luncheon and afternoon reception.''

''Are we staying Saturday night?''

''Yes, I thought I told you that. Mom and Dad were concerned about everyone drinking champagne and driving, so they asked everyone to stay. They've even planned a brunch for Sunday before we all head home.''

''Wow, that's some wedding. Expensive, too.''

''Yes, but his parents are contributing to it, and all of us kids are adding a little. Whatever we can. My brother Chance is the most successful, of course. He's been wonderfully generous to all of us through the years.''

James shot her a grin. ''That's what big brothers are for.''

''You have an older brother, too, don't you?''

He nodded, but seemed uninterested in talking about his family.

They'd been traveling about half an hour. ''I think the air is getting colder. Need the heater on?''

Startled, she pressed her hand against the window. It was definitely cold. ''Not yet. I'm comfortable.''

He leaned forward and turned on the radio.

Elise took the hint. She didn't want to talk to him, anyway, she assured herself. It kept her too focused on him. She leaned her head against the headrest and closed her eyes.

JAMES WATCHED Elise out of the corner of his eye, wanting to reach out and touch her. He'd kept his distance from the time he'd knocked on her door.

Tuesday night, she'd made it clear that she was still angry with him.

He longed to explain everything, to wipe the slate clean and begin again, as James Dillon, advertising executive, successful man-about-town, sought after, popular. Instead, she saw him as an out-of-work actor. He suspected she was still harping on Sandra, too.

Her touch-me-not attitude was driving him crazy. He dreamed of her at night. Hot, steamy dreams that left him dissatisfied when he awoke.

He hoped their hotel rooms were on opposite sides of the hotel. Maybe his would be next door to her parents. That would help him to keep his hands off her. He didn't want to do something with her she'd regret when she knew the truth about him.

But he had to get through the weekend first. It wouldn't be fair to tell her now, before their appearance in Flagstaff, when she might feel compelled to dismiss him before he did his job.

That noble thought almost made him laugh at himself. He didn't want to tell her the truth because he might lose her. And keeping Elise in his life had become the most important thing in the world to him. He had bought the SUV to please her...and himself. He could imagine all kinds of activities for the two of them where the vehicle would be better than the Mercedes.

Not that he was prepared to offer marriage. Not at this point. They'd hardly spent any time together alone. They should get to know each other better, he reasoned. But if she wouldn't speak to him after he came clean, it was going to be impossible to move their relationship to the next level.

After driving silently for some time, he realized she'd dozed off. Maybe she wasn't sleeping any better than he was these days. For the same reason? Could she be dreaming of making love to him? If so, he'd like to make her dreams come true.

He took one hand off the steering wheel and felt the box that he'd hidden in his sports coat pocket. She'd forgotten that little prop for their play. But he hadn't.

About forty-five minutes before they reached Flagstaff, he found a scenic overview looking across the mountains, pulled his vehicle into the side road and parked. The change of motion woke Elise.

"Are we there?" she asked, her green eyes dazed. "I'm sorry I fell asleep."

"That's not a problem. But we're not there yet."

"Then why are we stopping? Is something wrong with the car?" she asked, stress creeping into her sleepy voice.

"No, everything's fine. But I have something for you and I thought I should give it to you before we get to the hotel." He watched her carefully, but she didn't look enthusiastic.

"James, you shouldn't have gotten me anything. Your expense account isn't unlimited, you know," she fussed.

He stiffened. It was hard to remember he was supposed to have no money. "This isn't going on the expense account. You can give it back afterwards, if you want." Any hope for a romantic moment had disappeared. Instead, he was angry with her for bringing up the money.

Reaching into his pocket, he drew out the soft gray velvet box and opened it.

The ring was special, exactly what he would choose for Elise if he were really getting engaged to her. Instead of the traditional all-diamond ring, he'd chosen a large square-cut emerald with baguettes of diamonds in descending size on each side.

Elise gasped, staring at the ring, making no attempt to take it from its box.

"Don't you like it?" he snapped. It would be the final straw if she hated his choice.

"Like it? It's—it's spectacular. I've never seen such a beautiful ring. It can't be real!"

"Of course, it's real! I'd never offer someone a fake ring. That would be—" He broke off. He hadn't considered the cost of the ring. That hadn't been important to him. But he could tell it was going to be a problem for Elise.

"But, James, it must've cost at least ten thousand dollars," Elise pointed out.

Her gaze never left the ring, and the awed look on her face satisfied James. He'd chosen well. Of course, she was a little off on the cost. Triple her estimate and she'd be a lot closer.

Since she wasn't going to do so, he took the sparkling ring out of its box and reached for her finger.

She yanked it back. "No!"

"What do you mean, no? You like it. We need a ring for our story. What's the problem?"

"I can't accept that from you." Her voice was

firm, with only a slight quiver in it, and she turned away from the ring to stare out the window.

"Don't we need an engagement ring?" he asked, trying to be reasonable.

"It would've been nice, but I didn't think about it. We'll tell them we haven't gotten around to buying a ring yet. Now, let's go before we're late."

"Elise, you're being difficult. I have a ring. If you don't like it, we'll change it when we get back to Phoenix, but you—"

"When we get back to Phoenix, there won't be a need for a ring, remember?"

"Are you sure? What if you decide to let the engagement stand for a couple of months. Your sisters would ask what happened to your ring."

"That's why it's best not to have a ring. They'll think you're a terrible fiancé if you never buy me a ring."

"Well, I don't want them to think I'm a terrible fiancé," he said with a growl. He didn't like playing the villain. "Look, just wear the ring. We'll tell them it's my mother's, and you can give it back in a couple of months."

ELISE CAUGHT HER BREATH as he slid the stunning ring on her finger. It was a mistake to let him put it there, because she knew she was going to love it. She knew she'd never want to give it back. But—

A sudden, horrible thought struck her. "Is this Sandra's ring?"

He stared at her as if he couldn't believe her question.

"What?"

"Is this Sandra's engagement ring?"

"They're not engaged yet!" he snapped. "And I would never give you someone else's ring."

"Who is they?" Sandra had another lover? After all the time she'd worried about the young woman and James's feelings for her?

"Uh, my roommate. I tried to explain when she called the other night, but you wouldn't let me."

"Then why didn't she take the roommate to the party?"

"He had a prior commitment."

He shifted his gaze, and Elise, while she wanted to believe him, wondered if he could be lying. "James, please don't lie to me. You and Sandra—"

"There is no 'me and Sandra.' I have no romantic feelings for her and never have."

"But I think she does for you," she murmured softly. "The picture—"

"She was thinking about my roommate, I promise." This time he stared her directly in the eye, his voice sure and firm.

Elise's gaze fell back to the ring. "Is this really your mother's?"

"No. But it makes a good story."

"How could you afford it?"

"I got a bargain. And I made a down payment. I'll pay it out," he added with a shrug.

"For the next twenty years, I think," she whispered, still staring at the ring. "It's exquisite, James. I love it. But I'll take over the payments, I promise."

Suddenly he leaned closer and covered her lips with his. She still wore her seat belt, so their bodies remained separated, but his lips alone were enough to waft her away to the dreams she had each night.

When he finally lifted his mouth, after several drugging kisses, he said, his voice husky, "I'm glad you like it."

"I *love* it," she corrected, leaning forward to offer him her lips again. "It's unique and beautiful."

"I didn't know if you'd like a colored stone, but it reminded me so much of your beautiful eyes," he whispered before he kissed her again.

After several more minutes, he whispered, "Either take off your seat belt and let me hold you, or we'd better stop. I can't take much more without—"

"W-we'd better go on. I'll need to shower and change before the party this evening." She didn't want to stop. But in spite of his promises about Sandra, she still didn't believe they had a future. She'd be foolish to think they did when she was paying him for his performance.

He put the car in gear and pulled back onto the highway.

"By the way, the check I gave you hasn't cleared. You did deposit it, didn't you?" She'd balanced her bank statement the night before.

"Uh, yeah, I believe so. Sometimes my bank is slow. It probably got held up somewhere along the way. It'll be in the next statement."

"Okay," she muttered, staring again at her ring, turning her finger one way and then the other to see how the sunlight reflected off the emerald and surrounding diamonds. "It's so beautiful."

James's smile was his special one, and had the

same effect as his special kisses. She seemed particularly susceptible to both of them.

She looked up to smile back and caught a glimpse of something outside the truck window. "Uh-oh."

"What?"

"It's begun to snow. Look."

"Those are light flakes. Maybe it won't even stick," he suggested. "The ski area is higher than Flagstaff."

"Maybe so. Besides, all the activities are in the hotel except for the rehearsal and the wedding. But Flagstaff might be crowded if the skiing crowd shows up."

"But your sister made reservations. They'll hold the rooms," he assured her.

She certainly hoped so. After those intoxicating kisses, she knew she couldn't be in such close contact with James anymore. She crossed her fingers that their rooms would be far, far apart.

By the time they reached Flagstaff, the snowflakes were flying fast and furiously. They'd had to slow their pace because the streets began to get slick.

James pulled into the hotel parking lot with a sigh. "Glad we made it. I don't think the storm is slacking off at all. Put your coat on."

"Yes. I'm glad I packed several sweaters."

"You make a run for the hotel. I'll grab the bags."

"I could help you," she suggested, knowing her own bag was heavy.

"Nope," he ordered, leaning over to give her another quick kiss. "I'll get them. Don't slip on the snow." Then he jumped out into the storm.

Elise did the same and hurried toward the entrance of the hotel.

The first person Elise saw as she came in was the bride-to-be, her sister Sharon. "Sharon! What are you doing down here?"

"Elise! I'm so glad you made it. We heard the roads were getting bad," Sharon said, running to Elise's side.

Her greeting had alerted several other members of her family, including her parents. Soon she was surrounded, everyone asking questions at once.

James came through the door, his shoulders covered with snowflakes and his hands filled with their luggage.

Elise hurried to his side and brushed the snow off. He took advantage of her closeness to kiss her quickly. "Thanks, honey."

Feeling her face turn bright red, Elise faced her family. She hadn't planned that sweet moment, but it probably made everyone believe their playacting. She'd just opened her mouth to make the introductions, when Sharon screamed.

Looking around to see what had caused that reaction, she gasped as two of her sisters, Sharon and Melanie, grabbed her left hand.

"Would you look at that? It's gorgeous. Did James give it to you?" Melanie asked.

Before Elise could answer, her sisters and mother asked several more questions. Her father stood there beaming at her before he nodded to James.

"Evening, James. Glad you're here."

"Yes, sir, thank you. We are, too. The roads are getting slippery."

"Want me to help you with the bags?" Sam asked, still smiling broadly at James.

Elise was amazed at how comfortable her father was with James. Sharon's fiancé had spent more time with Sam, but he wasn't as friendly. It was probably because Sharon was his baby, the last to leave the nest.

James leaned toward Elise. "Should I go ahead and check us in? There's no line right now."

"Oh, yes, thank you, James. Do you want my credit card?" She'd meant to give it to him earlier so they could avoid this conversation in front of her family.

"Oh, they're all taken care of," Sharon hurriedly said.

Elise stared at her sister. She sounded nervous. Probably wedding jitters. Every bride was supposed to get them, though when she thought about marrying James—as if *that* would ever happen—she didn't think she'd have any doubts.

JAMES ESCAPED the crowd of Fosters and headed for the reception desk. It surprised him to discover the one Elise had called Sharon walking with him.

He frowned. "I can take care of this…Sharon, is it? You don't have to—"

"Yes, I do. You see, there's a little problem."

James came to an abrupt halt. "A problem?"

Sharon cast a frantic glance over her shoulder toward the others, and James got an uneasy feeling in his stomach. "What problem?"

"I had two rooms booked for you and Elise. I didn't want to ask if—well, if you shared, you know?

Mom felt better about your having two rooms. But then Michael's great-aunt decided to come at the last minute. I tried to get another room. Really, I did. But with the snow, the hotel didn't even have a broom closet available.''

"I don't think we'd like a broom closet, anyway," he said with a slight grin.

"I know," Sharon said, shuddering.

"I'm sure Elise won't mind sharing with Michael's great-aunt."

"Easy for you to say," Sharon muttered. "You haven't met her. Anyway, that's not a possibility. You see, his great-aunt never travels without her maid."

James thought he knew where this conversation was heading, and he didn't think Elise would be pleased. Hell, he wasn't, either. It would be difficult to keep his hands off her even in a crowd. If they shared a room, it would be impossible.

"Isn't there someone I could bunk in with? I don't think Elise would—I mean, she likes her privacy."

"Probably because none of us had any when we were growing up," Sharon told him with a grin. "It won't be so bad. I mean, you two are engaged. You've probably already— Not that it's any of my business," she hurriedly added.

They'd reached the desk, and James directed his question to the reservations clerk. "Do you have any empty rooms?"

"Oh, no, sir. Every available room has been taken."

"Can you recommend another hotel in Flagstaff?"

Elise would never forgive him if he didn't find a way out of this coil.

The clerk actually laughed. "No, sir. When fresh snow comes, so do the skiers. There's nothing available in a fifty-mile radius. We tried hours ago to find extra rooms, but they don't exist."

"Please, James?" Sharon pleaded. "We can't upset Great-Aunt Mabel. Michael said she's one of his most important family members."

He didn't know what to do. If he continued to protest, Sharon was going to question their engagement, which could reveal their charade. Finally, he nodded, managing a weak smile. "Sure, we'll be fine sharing a room."

"Thanks. Melanie said you were a good sport." She turned to the clerk and explained their reservation. In no time, James had been given two keys. A bellboy stepped up to take him to the room, but James decided he and Elise had best be alone when he explained their situation. Witnesses would not be a good idea.

When he started back across the lobby, Elise saw him coming and excused herself from her family, meeting him halfway.

"The party starts in half an hour, so we'd better get to our rooms."

"Uh, yeah," he said, hoping Sharon didn't feel it necessary to make an explanation now.

But she seemed no more interested in being present when Elise found out than he was in having her there. She kissed Elise on the cheek, and told her she loved her ring and she'd see her in a few minutes.

"The elevators are over here," James said, nudging Elise in that direction.

"Are our rooms on separate floors?" she asked, as they entered the elevator.

"Uh, no. We're both on the fourth floor."

"Oh. At least we're not on the top floor. I hate that."

Neither of them said anything else until the elevator stopped on the fourth floor.

"Which way?" Elise asked, stepping off. "What's my room number?"

"Four-o-seven. This way." He walked briskly toward their room. He didn't want to have this conversation in the hall.

They reached the door, and he handed her one of the keys. She slid the flat plastic card into the slot and pushed open the door to the room.

James had had his fingers crossed for two double beds. Instead, in the center of the room was a king-size bed. One king-size bed. They were going to have to share.

"This looks fine," Elise said with a sigh. "It sure beats being outside in that," she said, gesturing out the window where the snow was swiftly falling.

James set down both suitcases.

"You'd better go unpack, James. We don't have a lot of time."

He drew a deep breath. "Uh, Elise, there's something I have to tell you."

Chapter Fifteen

Elise was removing her coat, but something in James's voice halted her. She spun around to face him. "Tell me what? Surely you're not backing out on the arrangement *now?*"

"No. But your sister gave away one of our rooms."

"She what? Sharon?" When he nodded, she demanded, "What do you mean 'gave away one of our rooms'?"

He explained Great-Aunt Mabel and her accompanying maid.

"Did you ask for another room?"

"Of course, I did. I even asked about other hotels. It seems the town fills up when there's fresh snow."

Elise knew that was true. She sorted through other possibilities in her head and came up with precisely zero. She looked around the room and then back at James. "You mean you expect to share this room with me?"

To her surprise, irritation spread across James's face. "Look, it's not my fault. I tried to find another room. If I'd continued to protest, your sister would have started questioning our supposed engagement.''

''Our supposed engagement doesn't mean we're sleeping together!'' she snapped.

''We're not teenagers, Elise. Who's going to believe that we're engaged and not intimate?'' He stood there, his feet spread, his hands cocked on his hips, looking like a man in charge.

He was right. Who would believe she'd resisted this man if their engagement was real? Slowly she sank onto the edge of the bed. ''What are we going to do?''

The challenge went out of his stance, and he smiled ruefully. ''Share a room. Do I need to promise you—''

''No, of course not. I trust you, James, but—but it's not going to be easy.''

''Tell me about it,'' he muttered.

Elise licked her lips. ''Uh, I have to have a shower.''

''Yeah. I'll unpack while you do. Okay if I take the right side of the bed and dresser?''

''Of course,'' she agreed. She looked at the bathroom door, then at her suitcase. ''I'll get what I need from—or I can quickly unpack. That might be best.''

''Okay,'' he agreed. Without her asking, he swung her suitcase onto the bed.

''Thanks.''

For several minutes, each filled the drawers of the dresser with their belongings. Elise watched James out of the corner of her eye until she caught him doing the same thing. Blushing, she turned away, warning herself to stop being silly.

Quickly gathering up everything she'd need for her shower, she headed to the bathroom. "I'll hurry."

"I'm in no rush," he assured her. "I think there's a hockey game on television."

She gave him a brief smile and closed the door. Then she collapsed against it. It was going to be impossible to keep her distance from James when they were sharing the same room. The same *bed.*

She thought of the classic movie, *It Happened One Night,* with Claudette Colbert and Clark Gable. They'd shared a motel room, and Clark had strung a cord across the room and hung a bedspread on it to form a wall.

But they'd had twin beds.

That was it! Elise would call the desk and switch their room for one with two separate beds! She turned and swung open the door.

James was hanging up the phone.

"Did someone call?"

"No," he said as he shrugged. "I called the desk to see if they had a room with separate beds."

"I just thought of that," she said, smiling. "And?"

"Nope." His laconic answer didn't give her much information.

"No? Why not? There are lots of rooms. Surely someone hasn't checked in yet."

"I asked that. They said everyone came in early because of the snow."

Elise's shoulders sagged. "Of course. Well, thanks for trying." She backed into the bathroom and closed the door. A look at her watch warned her to hurry.

It wasn't until she was under the hot spray of the shower that she grew irritated.

"Why is he so upset about us sharing?" she muttered. "Is he afraid I'll demand more for my money than we agreed on?"

She knew her thoughts were irrational, but she couldn't make them go away. He shouldn't have been so anxious about it. She hadn't attacked him yet. He'd tried to reassure her. Maybe she should have reassured him.

As if she needed to!

When she emerged from the bathroom, her makeup perfect, her hair styled, her composure in place, she said, "I hope I don't need to reassure you that I won't make any demands."

He'd smiled when she started to speak. By the time she finished, he was frowning.

"What are you talking about?"

"I assumed you tried to find a room with two beds because you were concerned that I might expect...more for my money." She stood stiffly, staring out the window.

A chuckle filled the room—deep, enriching, complete. She turned to stare at him. "What's so funny?"

To her surprise, he crossed the room and took hold of her arms.

"You are."

She stepped away from his touch. "I was trying to reassure you."

"Elise, if you want to have your wicked way with me," he said, leering at her, "don't think I'm going to complain."

"You seemed pretty anxious to find us a room with two beds," she pointed out.

"Damn it, of course I did. I've given you my word. I thought it would make things easier on both of us. You already know I'm attracted to you. Crawling into the same bed with you tonight isn't going to change that. In fact," he said, pausing as his eyebrow rose, "it will make it worse."

She appreciated his concern. She really did. But a little corner of her heart gave a lurch in appreciation as he let her know he still wanted her. "Yes, I—I'm sure we'll manage, though."

He dipped his head for a quick kiss, then released his hold on her and stepped back. "Yes, we will. Until Sunday. All bets are off on Sunday."

She frowned. "Sunday, our pretense will be over."

"Yes. And when it's over, you and I are going to have a long talk."

"About what?"

He started toward her, then stopped himself. "The future, Elise Foster. We're going to talk about the future. Because I don't think I'm going to go to Hollywood. Not if I have to leave you behind."

ELISE WAS AMAZED at how well they managed. Even Friday morning wasn't all that awkward. James was in the shower when she awoke. When he came out, she went in with scarcely any conversation. He was waiting for her when she emerged.

"Good morning. Did you sleep well?" he asked, as she circled him, keeping her distance.

"Yes, thank you. And you?"

His gaze shifted to the bed. She'd carefully stored the extra pillows she'd requested in the top of the closet so the maid wouldn't remove them when she cleaned the room. She'd lined up the pillows along the center of the bed to provide a wall à la Clark Gable.

"Fine," he said, shoving his hands in the pockets of the gray flannel pants he wore, topped by a blue sweater and white shirt.

"You look very nice."

"Thanks. So do you."

"We're very polite, aren't we?" she finally said with a small smile. She missed the friendliness they'd shared at various times during their pretense. But then, maybe that friendliness had been a pretense, too.

"Yeah. Look, your dad called while you were in there," he said, nodding toward the bathroom. "He's invited me to a poker party, since you ladies will be tied up and we can't get out of the hotel because of the snow."

"Oh." She had to go to the bridal luncheon, which was actually a brunch and started in half an hour. "I'm sorry if it's not what you want to do. Want me to call Dad?"

"No. I wasn't complaining. I'll enjoy it. When will you be back?"

"I'm not sure. Mom said something about tying bags of rose petals for tomorrow's reception after the brunch. I might be busy most of the day."

She didn't want to be. James's words last night before the party had her anxious to spend time with him. To question him. To see if there really could be any future for the two of them.

He sighed. "Yeah, I figured."

"Do you need some money for the poker game?" she asked, wondering if sudden concern over the unexpected expenditure could be part of the problem.

"No. I'll be fine."

"Okay. Be sure you put it on your expense report."

Those words didn't make him any happier, if she judged by his expression.

"Yeah."

"I have to go now or I'll be late."

He didn't come any closer, much to her regret. No goodbye kiss for her.

Just a casual "See you later."

Had she misinterpreted what he'd said? Had she let her heart guide her instead of her head?

With an abrupt nod, she backed her way to the hotel room door. When he said nothing else, she opened it and left. She had no reason to linger.

JAMES SAT ON THE EDGE of the bed and buried his head in his hands. Damn, what was he going to do? Two more days spent in this room with Elise—and he'd promised to keep his hands off her?

He'd thought he'd never get to sleep last night, knowing that she was sleeping on the other side of the pillow lumps. The temptation to throw the pillows against the wall and slide his arms around her drove him crazy.

He'd been in a constant state of arousal.

Which explained the early morning shower. A little cold shower in the middle of a snowstorm ought to bring him back to reality.

Until he opened the bathroom door to see her sitting on the edge of the big bed, wrapped demurely in a white silk robe, her beautiful hair rumpled, her eyes sleepy. She looked like a virginal bride, waiting for his kiss to awaken her.

Instead, she'd rushed past him into the bathroom and shut the door.

Now he had to spend half the day sitting around playing cards. He enjoyed poker with the guys. Of course, he did. But how could he concentrate on cards when all he could think about was Elise?

He was going to get his clock cleaned.

"YOU ARE SO LUCKY, Elise," Roxanne, one of her sisters, gushed, leaning toward her. "James is such a hunk."

Elise smiled but said nothing.

"And he has such beautiful manners," Melanie added. "When I met him, Elise had just spilled cola all over herself. He still introduced himself. And he was very attentive to her."

"You spilled soda all over yourself?" her mother asked, staring at Elise. "How did that happen? You're usually not clumsy."

Elise wanted to tell her mother that it had been James's fault. But that would only lead to more questions. And she'd had enough questions for one day.

Before she could come up with an answer, Sharon giggled and said, "She must've had her mind on James. He's enough to distract any woman. Is he good in bed?"

"Sharon!" Margaret protested. "That's not a nice thing to ask your sister."

"Oh, Mom, move into the new century," one of her other sisters said. "She'd be an idiot if she hadn't jumped his bones at the first opportunity."

While her mother protested, her other sisters seconded that remark. Elise felt her cheeks heat, but she said nothing.

Aunt Lilly stopped the discussion. "Ladies, we need to finish our brunch. We still have a lot of rose-petal bags to tie. And your mother and I made appointments for all of you at the beauty shop for manicures. Tomorrow morning, you'll have your hair done. So leave Elise in peace and eat your lunch."

Dutiful agreement filled the air, and everyone turned their attention to the meal.

Aunt Lilly, seated beside Elise, leaned closer. "Your sister's right, Elise. You really are lucky."

Elise stuffed a bite of baked chicken in her mouth and chewed determinedly.

She had nothing to say.

"MAN, YOU ARE one lucky son of a gun," Chance Foster growled, as James raked in another pot.

James shrugged and gave a rueful grin. He couldn't explain why the cards were favoring him, but it was getting ridiculous. He'd even drawn a straight flush this last hand.

"Of course, he is," Sam, Elise's father, said with a laugh. "He's caught Elise, hasn't he?"

Michael protested, "I'm the lucky one. I'm marrying Sharon tomorrow."

Everyone agreed with him, even though he hadn't won a hand.

The door opened and several waiters rolled in carts bearing finger foods and sandwiches.

"Oh, good, lunch is here," Sam said, standing. "We'll interrupt the cards to eat a little. Maybe it will change the luck, Michael."

As everyone stood, Michael, the groom, looked at his watch. "I wonder when Dad will get here. I hope the snow didn't cause any problems."

"It ended about half an hour ago," Chance said, clapping him on the shoulder. "I'm sure your father will be here any moment."

James hadn't even realized the groom's father hadn't arrived. There were nine men in the room, two others Sam's age. He'd assumed one of them was Mr. Whatever-his-name-was. Frankly, he couldn't remember Michael's last name.

The door opened again and the missing father appeared. A father James recognized at once. One of the two state senators for Arizona: Senator Earl Gardener.

Fortunately, the senator wouldn't remember him. He'd met him once but he'd been in a crowd.

Michael proudly introduced his father to everyone. The senator looked at James. "Have we met before?"

"I don't think so, Senator. I'm not a member of the family," James said hurriedly.

"Not yet," Sam said, and winked at him.

James nodded at Sam, struggling to smile. His smile came more easily when the senator nodded and turned to greet someone else.

Whew, a close call. Another thought occurred to him. Where the senator went, so did the press. Surely they wouldn't follow him here, to a private wedding? Even if they did, they were probably all national reporters. They wouldn't know anyone from Arizona. Right?

He frowned, trying to remember if he'd ever met any of the national press.

"Don't like what you see?" Sam asked. "We can order something if you tell me what you want."

"Oh, no, Sam. This looks great. I guess I was worried about my luck changing."

"Shoot, boy, you've made enough off of us, you can lose the rest of the hands and still be okay."

"True. Unless we play all afternoon." He'd been hoping all this male togetherness might end soon so he could catch a glimpse of Elise. He missed her.

"Naw, there's a hockey game on ESPN at two. We're going to watch that. You like hockey, don't you?"

"Yeah, sure. That'll be great."

Chance stepped closer. "What are you two talking about?" He carried a plate loaded with food.

"I was telling James we're going to watch a hockey game later." Sam moved to the table, grabbing a clean plate.

Chance studied James. "You worried about something?"

"No, of course not. I'm having a great time."

Chance grinned. "I would think so. You must've won almost every hand."

"Not because I'm a great poker player, I can assure you," James said, shrugging.

"I know. Like I said, you're just plain lucky." Then he nodded toward the table. "If you don't fill a plate soon, though, you'll be out of luck…and extremely hungry."

James took the hint.

JAMES WAS FINALLY reunited with Elise when he returned to the room at a quarter to six. Since the rehearsal began at six-thirty, there wasn't a lot of time for chitchat. Especially since Elise was in the shower.

By the time she emerged, in a slinky green dress that clung in all the right places and exposed a great deal of leg, he was thankful for his time in the shower.

The rehearsal was standard fare, though there was a great deal of laughter when Michael stuttered through his part as he and Elise played the roles of bride and groom. Sharon had said it was unlucky for her, as bride-to-be, to participate in the rehearsal.

Elise had protested being the chosen one, but all her sisters had pointed out that she'd need the practice for her own wedding. Everyone turned to grin at James. Someone even suggested he stand in for Michael.

Sharon, however, refused that offer.

James sat two rows from the altar and watched Elise walk down the aisle, carrying some plastic flowers to simulate the bridal bouquet. It didn't take much imagination to visualize her coming to meet him as his bride. He'd thought never to marry again. Now it not only seemed plausible but a foregone conclusion. Someday.

He sat beside her at the rehearsal dinner back at

the hotel, his gaze drawn to the low V-neck of her dress. When Sam addressed him, his head snapped up and he felt his face flush. He only hoped the man couldn't read minds.

"Yes, Sam?"

"What do you think of the Coyotes' chances this season?"

James stared at him. The man wanted to talk hockey now? With Elise sitting beside him?

"Elise said you're a hockey fan," Sam said, looking puzzled.

"Uh, I go occasionally," he muttered. "But I'm not an expert."

"I'd like to know how you get tickets," Chance said, leaning forward. He sat across from them, without a date.

"I have a friend who has season tickets," he muttered, not wanting to get into a discussion about *that* again.

"You'd love them, Chance," Elise said. "They're right down on the ice. It almost feels like you're playing with the team."

"You got to go?"

"Yes, last Tuesday night."

Chance turned back to James. "I'm going to have to get to know your friends, James."

Fortunately, the subject of the conversation changed. Until dinner was over and the dancing began.

Before he knew it, James was holding Elise against him, barely moving to the slow, romantic music that filled the room.

"Are you doing all right?" Elise whispered.

Hell, no, he wasn't doing all right. He wanted her so badly, he could hardly move. "Uh, yeah."

"Did you meet Michael's parents? They seem very nice."

He gathered her a little closer to him. "Yeah. I didn't know his father was a senator."

"Yes. I hope Sharon's prepared for that."

"What do you mean?"

"The man draws a lot of publicity. So does his family. We've had several reporters here at the hotel, wanting to interview the senator, but they also requested an interview with the happy couple. I think that might get tiring after a while."

James was distracted from his hunger for Elise. "Did they go away?"

"No, I don't think so. But I'm sure they won't be a problem."

James had so many problems to deal with, what were a few scoop-hungry reporters? His major difficulty centered on the beautiful woman in his arms.

By the time they retired to their hotel room, he'd made up his mind. He immediately gathered up jeans and a sweater. He intended to wander the hotel lobby until much later, when he knew Elise would be asleep. It was the only way he could get through the night.

"What are you doing?" Elise asked, her gaze puzzled.

"I'm getting out of here."

"You're leaving?"

He hadn't been too tactful. He tried again. "Sweetheart, if I don't leave for a while, let you get to sleep, I'm going to— I've been holding you close all evening. I even drank a little champagne. I don't think my self-control is at its best.''

There. He'd explained his problem clearly. She'd let him leave now. She wouldn't protest.

''James, I don't want you to leave.''

Chapter Sixteen

The words popped out before Elise actually acknowledged the truth of them.

"Elise, I can't—" James began, scowling at her. Then he sighed and put down the clothes he had gathered up. "I'll try, if that's what you want."

"It is," she whispered, then licked her dry lips.

He groaned and turned his back.

"James, I don't think you understand." Either that or he didn't want to make love to her. She prayed he didn't understand.

"Sure, I do, honey, but you're the one who doesn't understand. It's not easy for me to resist making love to you."

"I don't want you to."

He spun around quickly, almost losing his balance. "What did you say?"

"You said you and Sandra weren't—"

"What does Sandra have to do with anything?" he demanded.

"I don't want you to betray any—any promises you've made." She took a step toward him.

"The only promise I'll betray is the one when I

promised not to touch you.'' He moved closer, too, and she could hardly breathe.

''I don't want you to keep that promise.'' She reached out, and he swept her into his embrace.

She drew a deep breath, taking in his aftershave, his maleness. His essence. Now that she knew he wasn't involved with Sandra, she could no longer resist him. Her arms slid around his neck as his lips covered hers.

She became lost in the magic, the fire, that swept through her, as it always did when he kissed her. But this time, having admitted her hunger, the effect was even greater. She never wanted to leave his arms.

She didn't know how long it took for them to move toward the bed. She hadn't thought she was in any hurry, but tension was building in her, a craving for the ultimate joining. A hunger for this one man.

Even as he moved her nearer to the bed, even as he struggled with the zipper to her dress, even as he kissed her senseless, it was James who tried to talk.

''Elise—'' he began.

Was he going to call a halt to what they were doing? She tightened her hold on him, returning her mouth to his. She wanted this moment, this loving, more than she'd ever wanted anything or anyone.

''I have to tell you—'' he muttered, pulling back.

He did want to talk. She couldn't believe it. As his arms left her, she reached for the zipper he'd been working on and slid it down.

Then she dropped her dress to the floor. The lacy bra beneath the dress had a front clasp and she snapped it open, letting the bra follow the dress.

She'd had no idea she could be so shameless.

James inspired her.

As she did him. With a gasp, he closed the distance between them, and his hands cupped her breasts. "You're so beautiful!" he whispered.

But his reluctance had irked her. She let his hands rest there a moment before she backed closer to the bed. "You wanted to talk?" She'd tried to sound cool, sophisticated. Instead, she sounded as if she'd just run a marathon.

James stepped closer. "Uh, yeah— I have to tell you—" He stopped talking when his mouth descended to her breasts and his arms pressed her to him.

"What do you have to tell me?" She was suffering. Why shouldn't *he?*

He raised his head and stared at her, a frantic look in his eyes. "I'm James!" he exclaimed before his lips covered hers.

The fact that his words didn't make sense didn't disturb Elise. She'd worry about that later. Now she had to strip a certain, delectable male. One she was crazy about. She reached for his starched white shirt.

By the time they actually landed on the bed, his shirt was gone and his pants weren't defying gravity any longer. And neither of them wanted to talk.

With all their clothing removed, James pulled her against him and his hands roamed her heated flesh, learning every curve and dip.

She returned the favor, finding the male physique more fascinating than she remembered. In between explorations, their lips clung together as they tasted of passion, desire...love.

When she urged him to complete their loving, he

slid from the bed and she thought she was going to die. He was refusing? He'd taken her this close to the edge but refused to show her paradise?

Her anger disappeared when she realized he was searching frantically for a condom. She hadn't thought of that. She was grateful he'd come prepared, because she didn't think she could bear it if they had to stop now.

When he came back to her, she welcomed him with fiery kisses and frantic urgings. He slipped between her legs, and he and Elise were swept up in a tide of passion.

Elise had never before experienced such a glorious blending of physical pleasure and emotion.

JAMES AWOKE some time later—he wasn't sure how much later—because of his chilled flesh. At least, the parts of him that weren't touching Elise. She slept beside him, a smile on her lips that filled him with pleasure. Their lovemaking had given him even more pleasure, but he'd feared she would regret what had happened.

He should have done a better job of explaining, he reminded himself. He'd tried, but Elise had been a little…distracting. He grinned as he remembered her striptease. Who would have thought conservative Elise would tempt him like that?

He only hoped she would do so again.

Even thinking about that moment made his groin stir. He shouldn't wake her. She'd need her sleep. She had to be up early for a hair appointment, at the ungodly hour of seven.

Even as he argued with himself, his hands, seemingly independent of his brain, began stroking her soft skin. His lips quickly joined in, and he felt her respond beneath him.

"Elise," he whispered.

She never spoke a word. Her hands and lips spoke for her. They told him she didn't mind being wakened in the middle of the night.

WHEN THE ALARM SOUNDED at six-thirty, Elise struggled to wake up.

"Honey, you have to be at the beauty shop in half an hour," that deep, delicious voice said. She couldn't believe an alarm clock had been manufactured with that kind of wake-up call. She'd—

"James!" she exclaimed, sitting up.

"Easy. You've got time."

"Yes." She couldn't think of anything else to say.

He took matters out of her hands as his lips covered hers and she floated back to their activities during the night. But only for a moment. He shattered those wonderful thoughts when he quit kissing her and scooted her to the edge of the bed.

"I don't like this any more than you do," he said softly, "but I don't want your mother mad at me when you don't show."

She smiled dreamily at him, wondering why her mother would be mad when Elise had just spent the most miraculous night of her life.

He prompted, "Sharon's wedding, remember?"

Oh, yes. Her sister's wedding. She got up and stumbled for the bathroom, hardly realizing she was nude until she saw herself in the bathroom mirror.

Reality slapped her in the face, and she gasped.

She'd slept with James. No, she decided, rephrasing that thought in her head. She'd made love with James. Wonderful love. Memories of what he'd done, what they'd both done, had her blushing, but not regretting her behavior. She'd learned a lot about herself last night. And about life.

Including the most exquisite pleasure that existed.

Making love to the man she loved.

With that thought singing through her brain, she stepped under the spray of hot water, delighted with the world.

When she came out of the bathroom just before seven, properly dressed but wishing she weren't when she saw James sprawled across the bed, she thought about kissing him awake.

But then she wouldn't want to leave.

Forcing herself to concentrate on the wedding preparations, Elise slipped out of the room, leaving her Prince Charming asleep.

She was the last of all her sisters to arrive. Opening her mouth to apologize, she was surprised when her mother sniffed at the air and turned her back on Elise.

"Mom, I'm not that late. They can't do us all at the same time, anyway," she assured her, laughing. Nothing could spoil her happiness this morning.

"Your being late isn't the problem. But keeping the secret from me when your father knew! I can't believe you wouldn't trust me!" Margaret cried, spinning around to glare at her.

Elise stared at her mother and then her sisters and two aunts. All of them were staring back at her.

"What are you talking about?" Had James revealed the truth? Had she slipped up somehow? How ironic that now that she and James were together, they were about to be discovered. No one would believe her happiness.

"I'm talking about this—" her mother exclaimed, jabbing her finger at an article in the newspaper.

Elise stared at it. Their pretense was in the paper?

"I'm talking about hiding the fact that you're engaged to one of the richest men in Arizona. I'm talking about James being the most eligible bachelor in the entire state! And you didn't even tell me. I can keep a secret, you know!"

Elise grabbed the paper from her mother's hands and stared at the printed words. It was all there. James's advertising firm, his incredible success. His brother Bobby, an actor at ASU.

They'd gotten confused, that was all, she assured herself. They hadn't— Her gaze moved to a picture of James, standing beside a young man who looked a great deal like him, only a few years younger. A young man she even recognized. He'd been in her class one semester. She couldn't have told anyone his name, until now, but she remembered his charm.

Quite similar to James's.

Humiliation washed through her, rinsing away the happiness that had filled her until that moment.

Melanie leaned forward. "You did know, didn't you, Elise?"

She gritted her teeth and lied as hard and fast as she could. "Yes, of course I knew. James— It was James's fault, Mom. He gets upset when he thinks someone likes him just for his money. He wanted you all to get to know him for himself before—before he told you the truth.''

Let James take the blame. Why not? He's the one who had lied. He's the one who had shattered her heart, making passionate love to her last night while he laughed about her naive proposition.

Making her believe in Prince Charming.

Phoebe was right. There was no such thing as Prince Charming. There was no such thing as perfect. There was no such thing as the man of her dreams.

James Dillon existed.

But who *was* he—this imposter she'd slept with?

JAMES SLEPT until eleven o'clock. When he finally stirred enough to look at the bedside clock, he couldn't believe his eyes. He hadn't slept that late in years.

But then, he hadn't ever spent the night making wild love to Elise.

He smiled, remembering their nighttime activities. Immediately, the idea of making love to her again...and again and again filled him. He would never grow tired of holding her in his arms.

Which led him to the next step.

He would marry her.

Even though he'd told himself he shouldn't hurry the relationship, should take time to get to know her, he knew that wasn't going to work. He didn't want time. He wanted Elise.

He was lying there, making plans, drifting into the future, when the phone rang.

''James, it's Chance. The females in this grand

production, including Elise, are all going to the church in the limo. Want to ride with me?''

James wanted to get to know Chance better. He'd rather be with Elise, but since that didn't appear to be an option, he agreed. ''When do I need to be ready?''

''I thought we'd leave in about ten minutes, to give ourselves plenty of time.''

''Right,'' James said, and slammed down the receiver. He had no time to waste.

In the end he was only a couple of minutes late; he was tying his tie in the elevator coming down.

''Sorry I'm late,'' he muttered as he reached Chance's side. He suddenly realized the man was dressed in a tux. ''Was I supposed to wear one of those?'' he asked, gesturing to Chance's outfit.

''Nope. I'm a damn usher,'' Chance said with a groan. ''I'm so good at it by now, I think I should rent myself out.''

James grinned. ''Don't worry, you only have one more sister to marry off, and that will happen soon. Then you'll be out of business.''

''You two have set a date?''

''No, but I don't intend to wait long.'' Once again, thoughts of Elise and last night filled his head.

''Well, I'll welcome you to the family,'' Chance said, grabbing his arm. ''At least you're not wet behind the ears like Michael. Getting married at twenty-two. Can you believe it?'' He dragged James after him as he headed for the exit.

JAMES WAITED for Elise's appearance.

He'd tried to see her before the ceremony, but her

mother had said they were keeping the gowns secret. She'd sent him on into the church. The dresses were all in lavender. Nice dresses, he admitted, as another sister came down the aisle. But he couldn't see any reason he should have been kept from seeing Elise.

She moved to the top of the aisle, and he caught his breath. He was sitting on the end of the pew so she couldn't miss seeing him. He eagerly watched her approach. She was so cute, taking her duties seriously, keeping her gaze fixed on the groom standing by the clergyman.

When she passed him, not looking in his direction at all, he frowned. She seemed—tense. It must have been because she was afraid of making a mistake. When she'd left him that morning, she hadn't had any regrets. He knew that. There couldn't be anything wrong between them.

Nope, everything was gloriously right. And as soon as he could get her alone, he'd make sure they had their own wedding as soon as possible. But he'd ask her to move into his house immediately.

As soon as he explained about his little lie.

ELISE HAD A PLAN. She didn't want a confrontation with James. Not here, where some of her family members might overhear. She intended to hold to her original plan, only instead of using Hollywood as her excuse for dumping him, she'd tell her family he worked too many hours, was too driven. She wanted a man who would concentrate on her.

Her family wouldn't be surprised.

And they'd never know about her lies.

She winced even as she moved to stand beside her

sisters and face the audience. She'd blamed James for lying to her. But she'd done just as much lying to her family. She had no right to paint him black while she cast herself in the role of the innocent.

She shrugged off those thoughts. It didn't matter. She'd get out of here as soon as the wedding was over. Without James. She had it all worked out.

She'd have her confrontation with him once she was back in Phoenix, away from her family.

While they'd been in the waiting room, a family friend of her mother's had slipped in to tell Sharon that she and her husband would have to leave immediately after the wedding, not even staying for the reception, because one of their children was acting the lead role in a school play this evening back in Phoenix.

Elise had followed the woman to the door, catching her before she could slip out, and had asked for a ride back to Phoenix. She explained that a friend in Phoenix had broken her leg and was in the hospital.

It was all arranged. When she got back to the hotel, instead of joining everyone at the reception, she'd race to her room...their room, and hurriedly pack, changing into her jeans. Then she'd meet her ride in the parking lot.

After a sweet ceremony that brought tears to her eyes—not because of her sister's marriage but because she knew she wasn't ever going to experience that moment with James—she crawled into the limo with her sisters.

She was sitting next to Melanie. As they reached the hotel, she hurriedly told her sister her made-up story, asking her to explain to Sharon and Michael.

Then she escaped.

Chapter Seventeen

James drove faster than he should have. But the snow had melted and the roads were dry.

And he was worried.

When he'd finally realized Elise hadn't joined her sisters in the receiving line, he'd asked her mother where she was.

"Elise? The receiving line just broke up, James. She's probably looking for you, you sly boy."

"I beg your pardon?"

"Oh, she explained why you didn't tell us who you really were, but we're not that kind of people."

He stared at her, heat climbing up his face.

Sam stepped forward. "She found out when they printed it all in the paper, James. Sorry about that, but I didn't tell."

Sam winked at him, and James hoped that meant he hadn't told about Elise's plan. But clearly her mother knew his true identity. "I apologize, Margaret. I shouldn't have lied."

"Oh, we forgive you, dear boy. After all, you're going to be family now. And compared to some of the things Chance did, your little lie was nothing."

"Hey!" Chance protested, stepping forward. "I'm innocent."

Both his parents laughed.

"Chance, have you seen Elise? I didn't see her in the receiving line." James watched him anxiously. If her parents knew about his real identity, he felt sure Elise did. She wouldn't be happy with him. Especially after last night.

"Nope, I didn't. But then, I didn't go down the receiving line. I headed for the food line. That was more important."

James smiled, but he started searching for lavender gowns. He caught up with one of the sisters. "Where's Elise?"

"You're still here?" she asked, surprised.

James couldn't remember her name but that didn't stop him. "Where's Elise?" he repeated.

"She had to go back to Phoenix. One of her friends had an accident and broke her leg."

"Which friend?" James asked, hoping the friend was someone he hadn't met. "And how did she go?"

"She didn't say. Maybe she took your vehicle."

James was pretty sure he'd left his keys on the dresser in their room. He excused himself and headed for the elevator. When he discovered the keys where he'd left them, he crossed to the phone.

Bill White answered on the second ring.

"Bill, this is James. Who had an accident?"

Silence was followed by a puzzled "I'll bite. Who had an accident?"

"No, Bill, this isn't a joke. Elise left the wedding early because one of her friends had an accident and broke her leg. Do you know who it was?"

''No, I haven't heard anything. I'll check, though. Want me to call you back?''

''Yeah, I'll give you fifteen minutes.''

Bill promised to hurry, and James hung up and started packing. He noticed the absence of Elise's belongings. She'd been thorough.

It was as if she'd never stayed in that room. Never made passionate love with him. Never slept in his arms.

Damn it, he hoped she'd panicked because a friend was hurt, but he was getting worried. Why hadn't she found him, asked him to drive her? How had she managed to leave without him? Why would she want to— Okay, so he'd lied about who he was.

But he hadn't lied last night. And he was going to tell her that as soon as he caught up with her.

The phone rang.

''Hello?''

''James, it's Phoebe. Bill's here and he said—''

''You're not hurt? How about Daisy, or Frannie? Surely it wasn't Helen?''

''James, none of us had an accident. No one is hurt. What's going on? Are you sure you got the right story?''

Coldness sank into James's stomach. He'd gotten the right story. But that was exactly what it was—a story. Elise had made it up to excuse her abrupt departure.

''Sorry, Phoebe, I must've gotten it wrong. Hope I didn't disturb you.''

''No, of course not, but where's Elise?''

''I guess she's on her way back to Phoenix.''

As he was now. He'd be back before dark.

And he had no intention of going home. No, he was going straight to Elise's. He intended to explain everything...and spend the night with her in his arms.

And the rest of his nights for the rest of his life.

IT WASN'T QUITE as easy as he'd planned.

When he knocked on Elise's door, Phoebe opened it.

"Where's Elise?" he demanded.

"She's not here," Phoebe said softly.

He didn't believe her. He slipped past her and headed for the bedroom. The first door opened to a bathroom. Empty. He reached for the other door, to Elise's bedroom, but he could see with a sweep of his gaze that Phoebe hadn't lied. He spun around.

"Where is she? Did she make it back okay?"

"She's here, James. I mean, here at Mesa Blue. Look, I don't know what happened. She wouldn't tell us. But she's very upset. She asked me to ask you to give her some time. She promised she'd talk to you in a few days."

James stared at her as if she had two heads. Days? He had to wait *days* until he could straighten everything out? Until he could hold Elise again?

"Phoebe, you don't understand!" he exclaimed.

She gave him an apologetic smile. "Probably not, but Elise is my friend. If she says she needs a couple of days, then I think you should honor her wishes."

His last flagging hope died a slow death. Phoebe was right. He loved Elise. If she didn't want to see him, he couldn't force her. At least she'd promised to see him soon. In a few days. But that would seem like an eternity.

"Okay, but tell her—tell her I can explain everything." He wanted to add, *Tell her I love her,* but he couldn't say that for the first time to someone else. It had to be Elise who first heard him.

"Tell her I'll call," he added.

"I'll tell her," Phoebe assured him, and held open the door.

Slowly, he trudged through it, the weight of the world on his shoulders.

PHOEBE STOOD at the window, watching James get in a dark green SUV and drive away, before she left Elise's apartment and knocked on the door next to Elise's.

Daisy opened the door. "Is he gone?"

"Yes, I watched to make sure. How's Elise?"

"Come on in. You tell me," Daisy said, a worried frown on her brow.

Elise gave the new arrival a bright smile. "Has he gone? Thanks so much, Phoebe, for doing that for me. I'll scoot next door, now, and be out of your hair. By the way," she continued in a chirpy voice, "how was your weekend? Any progress?"

Phoebe clamped down on her arm. "Elise, what's wrong? You're not acting like yourself."

Elise struggled to hang on to her composure. She'd promised herself she could break down as soon as she was alone in her apartment with no possibility of having to face James. "It was a stressful weekend. All those—lies," she said, and almost lost it. "I'm really tired. I'm going to rest now. Thanks again."

She slipped from Phoebe's hold and hurried to the safety of her place. Alone. She was finally alone. Riding back with her parents' friends, she'd endured constant chatter from the wife while the husband silently drove.

She had thought she'd go crazy.

She hadn't allowed herself to think about last night or this morning. Not yet. Because even a hint of either extreme of emotion and tears filled her eyes.

Now, no one would see her. She could weep for her lost love. She could mourn for what might have been. She could fall to pieces and no one would know.

She locked the door behind her.

"WHAT DO YOU THINK?" Daisy asked. Before Phoebe could answer, she added, "She was like that the entire time you were in her apartment. That brittle cheerfulness, that fake smile. I think she wanted to cry."

"I know," Phoebe said with a sigh. "I think she's going to have a major sobfest. But she doesn't want any witnesses. We have to grant her that, at least."

"But she's acting like her heart was broken. I thought they were just pretending."

"Method acting," Phoebe said softly. "We talked about it, remember? It looks like she fell in love while he was just pretending."

"Oh, how awful," Daisy said sadly. "What are we going to do?"

Phoebe shook her head. "I don't know. Check on her. Be there for her if she wants to talk. What else can we do?"

ELISE REMAINED in hiding from her friends at Mesa Blue for most of the week. She didn't answer her phone, either, ruthlessly erasing the phone messages James left every day that week.

Finally, she decided to stop crying her eyes out. She was being a royal pain to Phoebe and Daisy, shutting them out. They were her best friends.

When they called to ask if she'd join them for dinner at The Prickly Pear Friday evening, Elise surprised them by agreeing.

Once they were seated at their favorite table and had ordered their usual, she cleared her throat. "I want to apologize for my—my juvenile behavior this week. You've been very patient with me."

"Can you tell us what happened?" Daisy asked softly. "We've been going crazy trying to figure it out."

Elise was proud of her smile. It was small, but it was definitely a smile. And it didn't wobble. "It's not too complicated. I learned James had lied to me."

Phoebe frowned. "I thought you were the one lying."

Elise felt herself blush. "Yes, I was, but— Never mind. You're right. I shouldn't complain when he did what I was doing."

"What did he lie about?" Daisy asked, shushing Phoebe who'd also started to speak.

"He isn't James Dillon, actor and teaching assistant at ASU."

"He isn't?" Phoebe demanded in surprise. "But—but who is he?"

Elise drew a deep breath. "He's James Dillon,

wealthy advertising executive and the most eligible bachelor in Arizona.''

''But even Dave said he'd heard of him,'' Daisy pointed out.

''Dave said he'd heard of Bobby Dillon. He's James's brother.''

Phoebe and Daisy were speechless. Just then, George delivered their salads, so Elise turned her attention to dinner.

''But Elise, why— I mean, you were really upset.''

She tried a small laugh. It wasn't as successful as her small smile. ''Yes, silly of me, wasn't it? To get upset because— Since we were both lying, I shouldn't have— Oh, well, it's all water under the bridge.''

''But Elise—'' Daisy began.

Elise interrupted her. ''The good news, though, is that since James is wealthy and gainfully employed, he'll be perfect for your plan, Daisy. And I know you like him, so all you have to do is give him a call and all our problems are solved.''

She'd practiced that speech a number of times. She'd tried the vaunted method acting, trying to make herself believe that James and Daisy would make a great couple. She'd failed miserably at all of it.

''Don't be ridiculous,'' Daisy said, sending relief through Elise's veins even though she told herself she was being silly.

''I'm not—''

''Yes, you are,'' Phoebe said firmly. ''Have you told James how you feel?''

"How I feel?" Elise repeated, hearing the hysteria in her voice and trying to control it.

"Yes, have you told James that you're in love with him?" Phoebe asked again.

"No! No, I couldn't—I don't—"

She halted abruptly when Phoebe reached down and pulled *2001 WAYS TO WED* from her purse.

"Listen to this," Phoebe commanded. "'*Faint heart never won fair lady* is a statement that can be applied to females, too. If you have feelings for a man, stop hiding them. Let him know how you feel. If he doesn't return your feelings, you'll have a rough time. But the greater tragedy will be if he feels the same way and you're both too timid to let each other know.'"

"That doesn't apply to me—to us. James was acting. That's what I hired him to do."

"But he's not an actor," Daisy said. "You just said he wasn't."

"He's a natural," Elise said grimly, trying to shove away the memories of his rare talent.

"I think he loves you," Daisy said, staring at Elise.

"I agree," Phoebe seconded. "And I think you're being a coward not to tell him how you feel."

Elise wanted to protest. But she couldn't. She was a coward. But she also didn't believe he had any feelings for her. True, he'd called every day. But some men hated to lose a game. And she felt sure that to James that's just what she'd been—a game.

"It doesn't matter. We weren't at all suited for each other. I mean, Richard was a businessman, and that didn't work out."

"You can't compare the two," Daisy protested. "James is thoughtful, kind. And he makes you laugh."

Elise rubbed her forehead, feeling a headache coming on.

"And you can't deny the sexual tension," Phoebe added. "That spark Daisy's been looking for certainly seemed to burn brightly for the two of you."

Elise ducked her head, hoping her friends wouldn't notice her red cheeks this time. The spark had gotten completely out of control between her and James. And she'd finally admitted, toward the end of her torturous week, that possibly she had some responsibility for the night they'd spent making love.

After all, he'd tried to talk. Had he intended to tell her then? Even if nothing changed, if she never saw James again, Elise still couldn't regret that night. She'd learned about love in James's arms.

"I'm not suited to be his wife," she whispered. She'd given a lot of thought to this question, too. "I don't want to be a wife. I mean, I do want to be a wife, but that's not all." Almost desperately, she added, "I have a career. I don't intend to give it up."

"Did James ask you to do that?" Phoebe asked calmly.

"No! Of course not. We never talked about— It was always a pretense. We had no reason to discuss the future."

"Then, I think it's time you did." Phoebe sounded like a judge pronouncing her verdict.

HALF AN HOUR LATER, Elise couldn't believe what she was doing. At her friends' urging, she'd tried to call James. She'd discovered he had a housekeeper, MaryBelle.

When she'd started to hang up, the lady had said, "Is this Elise?"

"Yes," she'd answered cautiously.

"Lord have mercy, don't hang up. That boy is in terrible trouble."

"James? What's wrong?" Her heart had started racing at the thought of James in trouble.

"You—that's what's wrong. He's been trying to talk to you all week. I can't believe the minute he leaves the house, you call."

A small thread of happiness had tried to work its way through Elise's misery. "Where is he?"

MaryBelle had told her that James was at a formal reception in downtown Phoenix with all the important people in town. When Elise had told her friends, they'd insisted she join him. As had MaryBelle. It was a crazy idea, but the more she thought about it, the more she decided they were right. One of her concerns was that she couldn't carry off that kind of event. That she couldn't hold her own with wealthy, sophisticated people.

Phoebe had laughed and Daisy had assured her she could. Definitely, once they finished fixing her hair and makeup. She'd dressed in the green silk dress she'd worn last Friday night. Just before she'd made love to James.

It was her good luck charm.

"Wow!" Phoebe said, stepping back. "You look like a million bucks."

Daisy, having finished with her hair, urged her to the mirror. "Go look. Phoebe's right."

Elise stared at her reflection. "But I don't always look like this," she protested faintly. "What if James expects—"

"He's never seen you look like this, Elise, and he's still crazy about you," Phoebe said.

"You don't know—"

"His housekeeper said he was," Daisy reminded her.

They heard a car horn outside.

"The taxi's here. Come on, Elise, go get your man. Just like the book said," Daisy said. "After all, you're the one who bought it."

Like a zombie, Elise went down the stairs, got in the taxi and gave the driver directions. When he stopped in front of the hotel where the affair was being held, she almost told him to take her home again.

But she couldn't. Not when Phoebe and Daisy had prepared her. Not when they believed in her. Not when her heart still cried for James.

The admiring glances she received as she entered the room boosted her confidence. She scanned the cocktail party, looking for a handsome man. A particular handsome man.

"Dr. Foster?"

Elise whirled around, almost losing her balance. The voice was so much like James's, she was sure— But it wasn't him. It was his brother, Bobby. His arm was wrapped around a pretty young woman, the one from the newspaper photo.

"Hello, Bobby…Sandra. Is James here?"

"Sure is," Bobby responded. Before he pointed

out his brother, he said, "How do you know Sandra?"

"I don't, really," Elise said with an apologetic smile. "But I saw her picture in the paper, dancing with— Well, I thought it was James."

"Nope, she's all mine," Bobby said with obvious pride. "Show her your ring, honey."

Sandra blushed and extended her hand to show off her engagement ring. It wasn't the size of Elise's, but it was given with love, Elise knew. It also relieved the last of her worries about another woman.

"It's lovely. Now if you could tell me where James is?"

Bobby said, "The last time I saw him, he was by the food tables, chowing down. Which is good. He hasn't been eating much since—you know."

Elise didn't comment other than to thank Bobby. All those jealous moments over Sandra, and she was engaged to Bobby! It must have been him in the picture.

So James didn't have another woman stashed away. She felt reassured—until she saw him across the room, another blonde draped on his arm.

The temptation to run away was strong. But she wasn't going to be a coward. She hadn't answered his phone calls all week. If he'd found someone else, it was her fault. She squared her shoulders and slipped through the crowd.

JAMES HAD A HEADACHE.

His ex-wife, Sylvia, had been hanging on him, talking to him, ever since she'd cornered him fifteen minutes ago.

Incredibly, she seemed to think she could tempt him back into her bed. And she was still married to the poor chump she'd replaced him with.

"Come on, James, promise you'll come. Larry's going to be out of town all next week. I'll be…lonely," she whispered, leaning even closer to him.

He figured another inch or two and her breasts would fall out of her low-cut dress. Not that such exposure would bother or entice him.

His thoughts were only of Elise. He'd tried to speak to her every day. She'd promised to listen to him, but so far she hadn't honored that promise.

He was afraid he was going crazy.

He even thought he saw her now, here, walking toward him in that green dress that he'd never forget—

"James!" Sylvia insisted, tugging on his arm.

James attempted to shrug off her hold, but she wouldn't let him. So he dragged her with him as the vision approached.

"Elise?" he whispered, reaching out. Maybe he'd look like an idiot if she wasn't really there, but he had to know.

"Hello, James. I hope you don't mind my coming. Your housekeeper suggested—"

"MaryBelle? You talked to MaryBelle?" he asked, taking in what seemed an incredible mirage before him, smelling the perfume he knew he'd recognize from beyond the grave.

"Who is this?" Sylvia hissed, glaring at Elise.

"I don't mind," he said to Elise, ignoring Sylvia's question. "I'm glad. I've called—"

"I know. I'm sorry. I wasn't thinking clearly."

He reached for her hand, eager to touch her again. Sylvia jerked him back. "What are you doing?"

He frowned at her, wondering what she was doing there. He wanted to be alone with Elise. "Go away, Sylvia," he muttered, reaching again for Elise.

"No! I won't. Who is she?"

"I'm Elise Foster."

James smiled, his gaze gobbling her up. "Yeah, she's Elise." He reached for her again. This time, she extended her hand to him, and he clasped it.

"You can forget whatever plans you've made," Sylvia said. "My husband and I are together again."

"How nice," Elise said softly, her gaze never leaving James.

"So go *find* your husband," James said, sending his ex-wife a sharp look.

"I mean you!" Sylvia snapped.

Elise tugged on her hand, but James wasn't about to turn her loose. "She's making it up, honey. She's still married to someone else. And I wouldn't have anything to do with her even if she wasn't."

Sylvia shrieked something, attracting the attention of her current husband. He arrived to put his arm around his wife, but she shoved him away.

Which meant she'd had to loosen her hold on James.

He took the opportunity to pull Elise into his arms, his lips covering hers. Only Elise mattered.

Sylvia beating on his back distracted him. Raising his head, he realized the entire party had formed a circle around them.

Elise looked at him with stricken eyes. "I'm sorry,

James. I wanted to appear sophisticated so you'd believe I'd be an asset to your career.''

"An asset?" he muttered, frowning. "Elise, you're more important than my career. You're my life. I love you. I can't live without you."

"I am? Oh, James, I love you, too!"

He kissed her again.

"Stop it!" Sylvia yelped, while her husband tried to control her.

James raised his head again in irritation. "Woman, would you go away? I'm trying to kiss my future wife."

Elise stared at him. "You—you want to marry me?"

Flashes from several cameras distracted both of them.

Despite reporters pushing forward to ask questions, photojournalists snapping pictures, Sylvia still screaming and her husband shouting, James saw only Elise.

"Oh, yeah. As soon as possible."

"But, James, I can't promise to give up my career."

He frowned. "Who asked you to?"

"I thought—"

"MaryBelle's part of my family now, Elise. She'll take care of the house. We both have careers, but we'll put each other first. Everything will work out."

Her blinding smile was the only answer he needed. He kissed her again.

Jostled by the still grappling Sylvia, James whispered, "Let's go home."

Elise nodded, but she asked, "Can we go by Mesa Blue first? They're all worried about me."

James grinned. With Elise finally his, he could be patient. "Sure, we'll stop by there. Looks like my family has gotten a lot bigger."

That fact didn't bother him much, however, as he swept Elise into his arms and strode across the ballroom amid applause and laughter.

When they reached a black Mercedes, Elise stared in surprise. "Whose car is this?"

"Mine," he said with a sheepish look. "I borrowed MaryBelle's while we were—for the pretense."

"Why did you agree to my offer, James?" she asked quietly, after they were both in the car.

He sighed. "Well, sweetheart, I'd lost my enthusiasm for life. I was tired of all the women who wanted my money, who pursued me. I couldn't even get excited about work anymore. Then you came along, offering me a job, giving me a chance to be someone other than me."

He leaned over and kissed her.

Breathing rapidly, she pulled back. "Finish the story."

"I fell in love with you. You made life exciting again. You're perfect. I wanted to tell you the truth, but we were so far into the lie by the time I realized how important you were to me, I was afraid you'd send me away right before the wedding."

She nodded but said nothing.

"Why didn't you let me explain?"

"Because I loved you so much," she said simply.

James pulled her back into his arms and kissed her several times. When they came up for air, he asked, "Couldn't you just call Daisy and Phoebe? We'll go see them tomorrow. I don't think I can wait much longer to have you in my bed again."

She nibbled on her bottom lip, and he groaned.

"What about your housekeeper? Won't she—?"

"Nope, she'll be glad to see you. She says I'm a grouch without you."

"Okay, I can call them. I wouldn't want your reputation to suffer because you're grouchy."

"Sweetheart, with you in my life, I'll never be grouchy again."

He started the car and almost raced home.

By the time they arrived, Elise had forgotten all about that phone call she was supposed to make.

But then, her friends had read the final chapter of the book so they weren't at all surprised.

* * * * *

HARLEQUIN®

AMERICAN *Romance*

proudly presents a brand-new, unforgettable series....

TEXAS SHEIKHS

Though their veins course with royal blood, their pride lies in the Texas land they call home!

Don't miss:

HIS INNOCENT TEMPTRESS by **Kasey Michaels**
On sale April 2001

HIS ARRANGED MARRIAGE by **Tina Leonard**
On sale May 2001

HIS SHOTGUN PROPOSAL by **Karen Toller Whittenburg**
On sale June 2001

HIS ROYAL PRIZE by **Debbi Rawlins**
On sale July 2001

*Available at
your favorite retail outlet.*

HARLEQUIN®
Makes any time special®

Visit us at www.eHarlequin.com   **HARSHEIK**

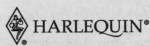

Harlequin invites you to walk down the aisle...

To honor our year long celebration of weddings, we are offering an exciting opportunity for you to own the Harlequin Bride Doll. Handcrafted in fine bisque porcelain, the wedding doll is dressed for her wedding day in a cream satin gown accented by lace trim. She carries an exquisite traditional bridal bouquet and wears a cathedral-length dotted Swiss veil. Embroidered flowers cascade down her lace overskirt to the scalloped hemline; underneath all is a multi-layered crinoline.

Join us in our celebration of weddings by sending away for your own Harlequin Bride Doll. This doll regularly retails for $74.95 U.S./approx. $108.68 CDN. One doll per household. Requests must be received no later than June 30, 2001. Offer good while quantities of gifts last. Please allow 6-8 weeks for delivery. Offer good in the U.S. and Canada only. Become part of this exciting offer!

Simply complete the order form and mail to: "A Walk Down the Aisle"

IN U.S.A
P.O. Box 9057
3010 Walden Ave.
Buffalo, NY 14240-9057

IN CANADA
P.O. Box 622
Fort Erie, Ontario
L2A 5X3

Enclosed are eight (8) proofs of purchase found on the last page of every specially marked Harlequin series book and $3.75 check or money order (for postage and handling). Please send my Harlequin Bride Doll to:

Name (PLEASE PRINT)

Address   Apt. #

City   State/Prov.   Zip/Postal Code

Account # (if applicable)   **098 KIK DAEW**